The Defector's Daughter

A thriller

John L Yahya Roberts

For Sonia

The Defector's Daughter

Acknowledgements

I am grateful to Touria Prayag at La Sentinelle Ltd Mauritius, for allowing me to use some adapted fragments of the first few chapters of the Defector's Daughter, that first appeared as a mini serial in the national magazine Weekly under the title the Bookseller of Budapest.

My special thanks to my long-time friends, Jim and Ginger Bernhard for their continued support, encouragement and perceptive advice on the development of the text.

I owe the inclusion of scenes of royalty in espionage to my daughter Dr Miranda Roberts, and also the title and some timely advice on teenage slang.

To Bilkis I owe my heartfelt thanks for her forbearance and love over the time of the unfolding of this debut thriller.

1. Operation Partisan

Partisan

HQCounterterror@gov.uk.org

Today 09.45hrs

You: Des.Archer@gov.uk.org

Execute a.s.a.p DB

Report back

M.O.

Partisan

Today 10.05hrs

Des.Archer@gov.uk.org

You: MO: HQCounterterror@gov.uk.org

Roger. Tonight

Des

2. Sara's Diary

Extract from Sara's Diary

I was having this really crazy dream. Got a meeting in the Senate House. Hurry. Take off converse all stars (of course wicked!) and shoot along barefoot. Could I get an amen? Look down I see I only painted one foot blue, the nails on the other still fractured red. Mugface. One of those phony buildings whose architect must have been on crack. No logic. Used to call this kind of junk existential. Some with stairs on the left others on the right. No shitty lifts, no through corridors, no windows, signposts, nor door numbers. Everywhere dim, dim: scary. Is that a thing? Then the dream went really crazy

'Hurry, hurry, you'll be late, mumbling.'
Then this fat, oops! weight-challenged guy says,
'Lost your marbles?'
'Fifth floor?' I ask him

'Here's the 6th, Miss, so you go up a floor to
the fifth.'
'Up. Not f...ing down?'
'Up. Up! Yer see, all the fifth is above 6th,
I'nit? Apart from the loos which are all on
the 7th. If they work. If you can find them!
Keep to the spiral stairs'
'Not where I come from, mister or what.
That's helical, goes up not flat, FWIW.
Spiral's flat, mister, see.'
The wonk continues in this strange dream.
'Never been here before?' Upsidedown
Senate: all downside up, yer might say. The
basement's a roof garden Miss, well they say
so: never been up there myself. Weird smell
they say: bats.'
Then he pissed off, sliding down the helical
banisters to the Penthouse doubtless. Cool! I
kick open one of the unmarked doors: no
door handles. Inside a theatre with the cast in
makeup and 18th century garb, Handel's
Water Music, vibrant in the background.
Someone shouts Curtain, and they all troop
of for tea or whatever, some certainly

embracing the moment or whatever on a dull
day.
'When do you open?'
'Open?'
'Yeah, your first night, Yaaaasss'
'Never have them; just rehearsals. More fun.
Audiences very odd here, 'Ye know! 'You
ever seen an audience Dapht?'
'Nah. Not Here: hate 'em'
Then in this oddball dream the next door
leads to an elaborate dining room set for a
banquet. Round tables for eight, set with
white linen, gold plated cutlery and crystal
glasses, five to each place setting.
Next room in semi-darkness, full of disabled
children, blind, deaf, legless, armless, one
with no eyes or ears. All screaming silently
as if their vocal-chords had been cut. OMG! I
close the door on that nightmare scene fast. I
go down a floor to find an Olympic sized
swimming pool, full with a class of pregnant
women, holding their tummies as if they are
saving their foetus from drowning. Hot and
clammy; steam rising above the water

11

*surface and the strong odour of chlorine and
sweaty bodies, one woman floating on her
back like a marooned whale or a fat Katy
after a bad hair day gorging 'til she throws
up. Omnishambles.*

*Then this dream just killin it, beyond the pool
are two wicked bronze doors, elaborately
fashioned, heavy and reluctant to be opened.
'Push hard Miss, they never quite got ehm
balanced and no power system on 'em either.
Not right. That. It's the cardiac patients as
feel it the worst. Can't shift them and need
help. So, my young Galahad here, me son,
gives them his shoulder…'*

*Beyond the doors, down marble steps, a
garden maze of bamboo and at the centre, I
contrive to see a carved fountain with doves
and snakes and nymphs. Dancers in bee-bop
dress, prancing up to their nipples in the pool
about the fountain. OMG!*

*Then the janitor returned
'Lost again Miss? Never find what yer
looking for here…everyone's the
same…lost…just keep getting lost. No hell*

*fires, just forever lost and hurrying to
something that never is or was or will be…
Just how I feel often these days, just lost and
missing my mum and wondering if I'm
normal…' Then the dream went on a bit…
A gardener approached me wearing boots
with fashioned spaces for his toes, like gloves
on his feet. He speaks in a strange language
and strides up to me wielding a steel spade. It
catches me behind the right ear. I fall to the
ground, covered with cherry blossom from
the trees in full flower and topiary above
shaped into game birds; Chill! One is a
peacock with a brightly fanned
tail…unconscious for how long I cannot
tell… a minute, an hour a day, a decade or
one hundred years… who can tell? But still in
time for my senate house meeting if only I
could find the way!*

These are the first pages of the diary of
Sara the strange one. They thought she was
autistic. Her jottings from a recurring panic
dream. She always reads these before making
another of her entries scattering parts of her

story with her defecting father for her fresh found friends Emma, Katya and Chloe, the only ones she half trusted to keep her secrets, except those multitude of truths of her short life that she could confide to no-one but herself. For, she felt now pledged to levels of secrecy that would put in danger not just her life and her father's but many beyond her knowledge secluded from each other in this obscure world of mysteries and most foul deeds.

This entry in her journal marks the close of her deep depression, when she thought she was just mad. Sometimes she just wanted to end it all. In the garage with the engine running and a rubber pipe in the car connected to the exhaust: headache; nausea; unconscious; dead. She had Googled it many times and linked with others in Instagram with the same mental health issues. Anxiety, doubts about whether she was insane, bio, bonkers.

Then that very day, it all changed. That moment. There. The mutation. The metamorphosis. The liberation. The total ungluing. There within the white walls of that young school doctor's sick-bay. Scarcely a year ago. That flash. Finding herself deep down. Normal, fresh, alive, new, bold. Gone that timid resentful, psychologically sick child with all those fears. Then the escape into a pulsating new world, released from the incarceration of her glue ear infancy, where all was friendless, a blur of sound, none making sense. Her world has been one of merely hiding in the shadows of her mind: bent just on numbers and their sinister spell over her. She was twelve. A child transforming into a woman. She could feel it and see it on her fingers, the red show of womanhood approaching fast. Sara was ready now for life at last!

Now, she looked up on the wall above her head to check that the Turkish scimitar was still in place, that her great grandfather had been presented after a memorial service for those lost at Gallipoli, Turks and allied military forces, fighting for and against access to the underbelly of Europe. Then she would sleep 'til her new dawn, shriven again.

Sara had been talking to Maryam about ISIS, the women and the men. She supposed they dreamt of a pure Caliphate. Dreams were primordial for her too. Couldn't live without them: could die for them. They must have thought all in ISIS would live a full Muslim life in peace and prosperity, enriched by the company of other true brothers and sisters and other women by their right hands possessed, the booty of war to convert and bear children. And then there was all that oil. No need to work and slave as before. But they were assailed by infidels who refused to convert, even after the hardest persuasion and just had to be made examples of to encourage the others. Yet so many beheadings.

Surely there was another way of tolerating all peace-loving minorities who paid their way. Wasn't it a faith built on peace and love? Maryam had smiled explaining that the young idealists were ignorant, many scarcely literate and were just told the texts from the Koran that told of the early times when western countries did not exist bound by human rights, the United Nations philosophy of peace and the notion of war crimes was just then in the future. Even though it was Saladin who had formulated a concept of peaceful coexistence and the ethical treatment of captives hundreds of years ago based on the early practices in Medina. The ISIS practice of death to the infidels by beheading or crucifixion of infidels was an outdated extremist view wholly rejected by the progressive Muslims where Maryam had lived with her family. Many Christians and Jews were her family's friends and neighbours. Live and let live had been their watchwords.

Sara closed her eyes. She lay down on the cold stone inside the mausoleum she had designed for her father, above his grave. It was 2.30 in the morning. Her last night to be with him She wrote a final entry in her diary, which had been her best friend since she had been given her first green leather-bound volume for her seventh birthday by her father. It had a clasp and a key and these were her most secret thoughts, which she had first meant for her children and grand-children, after her own death. But now, for whom? Posterity! She smiled at the self-indulgent thoughts. She would leave this last diary on the stone where she sat, for the next prayerful wayfarer who would discover her cold as the very stone.

Now all her evil thoughts of enemies in the past, even the suave traitors from within, all gone. Some never to be found. She closed her diary, illuminated by the rays of the full-moon above the stained-glass window. She breathed in softly the aroma of the vellum pages, and longed to open it again: but knew now what she must do. It was the very moment of time each night when flights took off to take the brave behind enemy lines. She recalled the images from books and films of the darkened faces of so many good men and women and their silk parachutes, some destined to horrible death of many whose secrets would die with them, as would hers. This was her final sanctuary. Where she had often come to commune with her father about her brief life following in his footsteps through a dark existence of clandestine action, trusting no-one.

She lay down on the cold stone. She inhaled the dank odours of this unlit place, where the sun rays could never reach and where the moon beams were faintly relieving the darkness of the recesses of the resting places from which no traveller returns.

Sara unpicked the lining of the cuff of her jacket. Extracted that pill, kept for just such a time. She placed it on top of her journal by her side, peering at it as it glistened in the ghostly moonlight. Yellow or white she could not see. A relic of her father's service training. She wondered if it had passed its shelf life and would still do the job. She had yearned for this atonement. For she had for some years feared the brutality of her father's jailer, Noah with his fierce art of dismembering the living captives. For him stoning and crucifixion were too vulgar. Flaying was more to his taste of barbaric cruelty…

Now Sara's pulse quickens as she feels a faint zephyr across her cheek, and sees a ghostly shape, looming over her, alighting on her right shoulder. She tries to touch it, but it eludes her hand, deftly streaming through her fingers, softly wailing and with a faint scent of lemon grass. It again comes towards her, a cowl hiding its face, no limbs she can see, just a fragile, gossamer veil encompassing it all and a quiet wailing as if it were lost.

'Stay!'

But it evaporates as noiselessly as it had come, dissolving into the faint moon beams that softly illuminated the dark cell and in a scarcely audible voice, whispers,

'No, no, not yet...Sara'

'His voice!'

'Father!'

Gone.

Only the faint scent of lemon grass remained amidst the dank odours of the mausoleum.

3. The Execution

The massive black hooded figure raised his sword, severing Zac's life, wrenching his head back, exposing his gaping gorge, jetting blood in a vertical pressured bright red stream, dousing the cackling executioner. The camera whirred as others, kneeling, bound and blindfolded captives, awaited the same end, for not converting. David Brand watched the video again which closes with a curiosity: the initials MO. He could have been there with Zac, his friend-in-arms, whose head hit the ground, with his lips still moving, in contempt or prayer. Who knows? Maybe only MO.

David packed his bags for another trip in his bizarre calling, now, himself, freed from the touch of war and grisly retribution. Yet his house was so infused with enticing scents, freshly cut flowers, cinnamon biscuits and the sound of sea gulls fluttering over the scraps left on the lawn from breakfast, that he yearned to postpone this persistent time for departure.

'Stay and cultivate your garden.'

Yet he could not follow those rational voices of his inner self. Not now as he packed to go again on another fruitless mission. For what? For whom? He peered into the shaving mirror, tracing the lines of his pale face and the bags under his clear blue eyes. He ruffled his tight sandy brown hair with tinges of grey at the temples, checking his teeth for further signs of decay. He groaned at his unkempt finger nails seldom taking time to trim them. He just no longer cared. His past was absurd: his future likely to be worse.

David was now forty-six, educated at Marlborough. He had had opted for Dartmouth with the Royal Navy, spending three terms at the University of Sussex studying Arabic, mathematics, cryptology and social anthropology, passing out as an officer in communications and intelligence services. He was then assigned to the British Embassy in

Cairo as military attaché and onward and upward with NATO in Paris.

He had been pressed to publicly resign as lieutenant Commander to join the freshly minted, clandestine, Inter-text International Academic Publishers Ltd, where he now worked in the European office setting up agencies in Tallinn, Estonia and in Budapest.

He had married Sandra Jamess when he was 23, a former classmate at Sussex. Their one child, Sara, was awkward and had been diagnosed in Egypt as mildly autistic.

Extract from Sara's diary

5 May 20–

It was wicked having him back. So close, But OMG he's gone again and I do fear forever. Hugged my teddy bear – much neglected. Needs a new button eye. And they want me to do all that kind of stuff after Russell. Hush! Hush! Cloak and dagger in your throat. Met Chloe at a gig last night: said all that was awesome. Just raved on and on in her blog. She really has mental issues, always on about

Mekkk and Safiya. Not for me and Teddy she does not think they're solid either! Might have more of his stuffing knocked out of him. Think I'll cool off with some Sophie McKinzie.

David now embraced the full naval set of beard and moustache; he had delicate ears and aquiline nose. He might have been mistaken for an ageing actor or film director. He kept himself fit, yet he was conscious he was losing his former erect stance and his muscular body from navy training, glancing in mirrors and shop windows to check the decline. He missed his former regular partners in squash and tennis. His relaxing cross country running was largely a memory. His complexion was increasingly lined, if perennially tanned from foreign travel and time at sea. He talked in a low musical baritone voice ever watchful for revealing the unintended clues of his covert calling. He had small feet, long slim fingers and, when he was younger, people had thought of him as smart and well kempt: but times were changing and he was letting things go, with the feeling he was past his best and no longer cutting the mustard at home or abroad.

David and his wife Sandra used to be taken as a socially favoured couple. But these days they whispered that he was going irreversibly down-hill: he seldom wore a tie and worked in his bookshop with rolled shirt sleeves, a loosely fitting waistcoat, and tight dark blue corduroy trousers, with a perpetually tired and anxious look, as if he was fearful of some impending profound loss. His former passion for classical music and traditional jazz was waning. In his younger years he had loved hill climbing and sailing, which Sandra now could not endure.

As David thought of all those student books neatly lined on the oak selves in his bookshop in Budapest, he mused that in his younger days he had been considered by the Navy, one of the best in small yacht racing at Cowes, winning many prizes. But his weak spot was Turkish delight and those honey baklava pastries. Had this been the cause of his gradual decay, and the pink gins and those dark fears?

Sandra kept cajoling him for his flaws. Was his sharp wit eluding him now? Was he past even a mid-life crisis of rejuvenation? Or was he just scared by the life in which he felt trapped with all its inherent risks of brutal encounters in shadowy places and the continual supervision of his bods who did most of the fieldwork and who just disappeared too often, too soon, to the inherent risks of the counter attack.

Another trip; another goodbye: another year frittered on the way. Then in those sweaty moments of intimate embarrassment that came to him more and more, he muttered,

'Fool! What are you doing with your life? Not fair to Sandra, nor to Sara. Are you going crazy? Or just crazy already...?

'She's not all there, really,' Sandra kept explaining.

Sara talked late and despite all that expensive tuition seemed to make little progress except in rebellion, tattered clothes, and her green stained hair coiffed to a peak. David was hardly ever at home. First it had been the navy across the globe and now world-wide marketing of text books with Inter-text, a seemingly smart academic publishing house based in Copenhagen, where they had been living for some years. Now off to Budapest.

Sandra had never been to his office, nor been invited, nor wanted to be: it all bored her to tears. Good pay, but books, books, when there was real work to be done? And then there was the other side of it, with David groaning in his sleep as if he was being beaten black and blue.

Sandra had been an executive, a fast-track high flyer in a liberal construction firm, as a civil engineer, taking safe water and sanitation to the poorest countries, mainly in Sub-Saharan Africa. Before baby Sara came, she had been always chic, as a counterpoint to her technical job, admired by the young studs. Now she was merely a frumpy fulltime housekeeper who never turned the lads' heads in the street; merely a carer for poor Sara and her other child, David, himself, who had never seemed to grow up since he joined the navy straight from school and had become totally engrossed in communications systems.

They had met in Sussex, when he was on a special course from the Navy there, became lovers and married after living together for four years, It was only after those sweetly fulfilling years, furthering her career and meeting David's demanding needs on his leave from his perplexing travels abroad, that she had found to her surprise, Sara was well on the way.

Sandra had been proudly fashionably smart, dazzlingly attractive with a professionally disciplined mind, not suffering fools gladly but always distinctly socially charming. Five feet six tall, auburn hair, green eyes, preserving her slim figure with a strict regime, she had been eye-catchingly rounded in the most feminine places, which she proudly displayed whenever in company.

Sandra still took care of herself, dressing assiduously for every occasion, yet having about her that unnerving scent of a once stunningly stylish woman seeking escape. She had a well-practised courteous manner, with those cultivated warm looking smiles of a mature theatrical public relations agent. But coupled with her rather short fuse, when domestic and social issues frustrated her, only too often these days, she had found this and the frequent changes of location, determined by David's peripatetic assignments, had increasingly diminished the range of her enduring contacts. She was rather ashamed that she only operated now in a tiresomely restricted social network of David's work friends, staff and parents at Sara's school, a dwindling number of former professional colleagues, two or three school and university class and room-mates and occasional distant contact with her first and former lover from Sussex, before David, whom she couldn't entirely dismiss from her longing dreams of a better more exciting tomorrow.

Sandra realised more and more her age: she was forty-three now, silently weeping at those past years of florid personal blossoming, with that rapid career growth that she had so relished in her twenties and fervently hoped whenever the phone rang that a new voice would call her to end that furtive searching for a new stimulating life beyond the house.

She had loved David once. It had been the great romance of her life. She had admired his strength of purpose, his quick wit and firm response to her passion. But that faded fast as he became more absorbed in naval intelligence work and he no longer confided in her about his strange pattern of travel, nor did they talk about those gruesome nightmares that seemed to trouble him more and more in the dark hours of the night, leaving him sweating and on the verge of tears. She had rather curtly decided to abandon him emotionally to his secret life, whilst trying without great aplomb to act the dutiful wife and mother, no longer having that part of her life cherished in her heart.

Sandra felt cramped in her current role as mother and wife and was longing to be back in her former business world. Having her only child, Sara, was immediately a shock, which she saw as an error of passing passion overwhelming her in a wayward hour. Her more rational self, silently regretted it every day, morosely trying to do her duty to provide the essential support her dependent and alarmingly volatile daughter demanded and hold on to the last vestiges of her fast-unravelling respect and affection for her husband.

E-mail to Des Archer

Partisan

HQ counterterror@ gov.uk.org

Today. 10.28 a.m.

des.archer@gov.uk.org

Close in T3, bait for Budapest.

M.O.

Desmond picked up the encrypted phone and called his asset in Hounslow. 'Angel? T3 13.25 BA for Budapest. Bait for target as before.'

'Confirmed. On my way.'

'She's not dyslectic, you know, I mean mentally handicapped or a miraculous savant, just a tie: she is just emotionally up-tight.' Sandra was explaining this to yet another new neighbour in their nomadic life, the strangeness

31

of Sara. 'Probably get over it in her teens. For now, you see, I'm her Mum, her home tutor and her friend. I mean, hope so. David's off to Budapest, isn't he? Back next week, should be, hmm, books for kids. That's his line. Bit far removed from the navy. But that's life, I suppose. The thing is…just hope he doesn't get caught up with all those desperate, pitiful war refugees from North Africa…'

David hugged her, passing a note to his driver, as he slumped into the back seat of the company car off to Kastrup airport.

'See you next week: I'll give you a buzz when I get there. Budapest, this time: book fair. Bye, darling, give Sara a kiss from me!'

They had worked from their base in Vester Brogade for some years now. Copenhagen, Sandra found, was in a kind of safe time-warp; it was a stately quiet city where people could play at romance in the Tivoli gardens with its restaurants, promenades, its concert hall holding a regular Carl Nielsen programme, all the fun of the miniature fair, its helter-skelter and musical carousel and happily a plentiful array of recharging points for their mobiles.

Sandra was the only child of a stockbroker in that far gone age when stockbrokers were decisively respectable, straight and well off, though rather boring. Her mother a politician manqué, had been into every conceivable voluntary group, for unmarried mothers, abandoned children, illiterate adults and stray dogs; on committees galore and a founder member of a madrigal group to boot. Sandra rather abandoned at boarding school in Oxford saw little of either of her parents except on summer holidays abroad. On other holidays, too often, she was confined to school under the charge of the matron who would take her to art galleries on her day off and on Sundays to evangelical Christian services.

At first, with Inter-text, David had been assigned to Tallinn, the former Russian naval base in Estonia, where, he had told Sandra, the sales of the new technical student texts on astrophysics and electronic engineering had been going well for the company. That was the official line anyway. She was not so sure.

As he waited for his flight, David worried about what Sara has said to him yesterday, as they had played tennis at the club. An item on the local news about his friend from Portsmouth, Desmond Archer, who had been arrested, bird watching with his powerful binoculars, in the wetlands, too close to the navy experimental rocket launching base. Better watch-it. Slip-ups like that are not helpful. Yet Desmond always had that touch of the masochist about him.

Desmond was different. David was never quite sure about him. Was he a friend, a competitor or maybe even…No how could that be? But trust no-one, David thought. Desmond was very bold in his approach to his work, always coming up with new outlandish schemes, like getting an agent on the inside of St Peter's in Rome, or putting a tail on the Duke of York, who he said he thought was a rogue and a risk to the monarchy. At school at the age of fourteen Desmond had gained an early place in the First XI cricket team being a hard hitter and fast bowler who could swing the ball both ways. He had become notorious for challenging the distinguished elderly cricket coach Jack Edrich, on the correct batting technique for dealing with balls wide of the off-stump. Edrich had unquestionable technical rules, after playing in 60 international Test matches against the world's best bowlers. His legendary favourite advice, 'No cutting or hooking before lunch on the first day,' had become a chant around the school playground. 'Then, he would add, 'if you have scored under fifty, leave the wide ball and shoulder arms: after you have fifty on the board, you are permitted to cut the wide ball downwards past the slips for a single to third man.' He usually said this with a sniff and rasping cough from sixty years of smoking Player's Navy Cut.

Desmond decried this cautionary approach and introduced the then shocking shot of uppercutting the ball over third man for six. He knew that opposing captains placed fielders at third man because they could not catch, or to give fast bowlers a rest who were not inclined to run fast to save boundaries off someone else's bowling. Desmond leaked his views to the local cub reporter on the Chichester Herald who promptly reported it in his next cricket round-up of local school matches. Desmond had scored three sixes and a four with this technique, after he had only 10 runs to his name on the board, before he was caught behind off a very thin edge, attempting another upward cut. He had been wildly cheered by his team and the few spectators for his thrilling innings of 32. Edrich was umpiring and had given Desmond out with doom written all over his face. Desmond was summoned to Edrich's room on the Monday morning and hauled over the coals. 'See, my son, only thirty-two when you could have gone on to get a ton. No cutting or hooking 'til you have fifty on the board and none of this suicidal upper cutting. Do I have to repeat the rule time and time again, 'til it gets into your thick scull' Desmond was sent to the nets in disgrace for practice in the evenings all that week to iron out his risky ways and dropped from the First XI.

He became a local hero. The news went viral round the schools and Desmond was nicknamed Daredevil Desmond and cheered on when at last he was given back his well-deserved place as an attacking opening bat for the school First XI. The practice of upper cutting was not long after to become a standard textbook stroke in county and international cricket. The name Daredevil D, stuck with him when he entered the navy.

After his training days at Dartmouth, where he first met David and Zac, Desmond was noted for reintroducing the heroic style of the Nelson touch in his student battles, deploying the latest GPS and sonar depth sounding methods. Thus, he could infiltrate his fleets inshore of the enemy, and turn a blind eye to signals from the commodore in the heat of model computer war games. When he transferred to the Naval Intelligence Services, he adopted enhanced interrogation of prisoners in the Middle East encounters and showed reluctance to take prisoners unless they were persuaded to be turned as double agents.

Desmond was born in Belfast and had been orphaned at the tender age of two years in the Troubles when his catholic parents were assassinated in front of him.by an extremist masked Protestant group who raided their house in error believing it to be an IRA safe house. Desmond was shot in the ankles and knees, but heroic orthopaedic surgery saved him from being a life-long physical cripple. But in his infancy, he became haunted by the event, his mind transfixed playing back the scene; as he reached adulthood, he became more and more focused on how he could avenge his parents' execution. It was no relief for him when he was put up for adoption and taken in by a very kindly Protestant couple who had not been able to have children of their own. He became almost mute, never losing his inner sense of despair for losing his parents and further resentment for losing his forename Patrick and his real father's family name Murphy and the enforcement of the new forename Desmond and his adopted father's family name of Archer. The final cut was to be brought up as a Protestant and to go to an Anglican church service three times on a Sunday.

He guarded all this rebellion in his heart. When he joined the Navy and was enrolled at Dartmouth, he sought out a Catholic chaplain, Father Paul Maguire. He started regular instruction, and took the three sacraments. Father Paul Maquire also initiated him in the IRA, being a stout activist native of Belfast and brought up in the St John's Parish Church on the Fall's Road. At Dartmouth Desmond, a name he still used, by habit and a kind of cover, linked up with Zac and David as mates and though they followed different paths remained in close touch and were drawn together on Intelligence operations.

Desmond had never wanted to be a British patriot, his aim was to seem to be on-side, but he nursed a secret ambition to betray them all, to get his revenge on the arrogant protestant Brits who had stolen his youth and murdered his parents before his very eyes. He could still see their warm blood seeping over the floor with its sickly odour. He could no longer weep for them. His tears had dried up long ago. His profound loss was now his spur to dark thoughts of reparation. He would remain low as a sleeper 'til the time was ripe. So, he became an easy prey to Mellissa, who sensed his duplicity and he became rapidly under control, prepared to follow her most brazen commands. Until the time was ripe: as ripen it was to be.

As David scanned the airport lounge, he mused on Desmond's strange story, which he had heard many times, and he smiled at the recent escapade, so much like Desmond to be caught by the police bird watching. Then David abruptly winced at the bulk of a foreign looking figure in the lounge, gorging into the Danish style herring open sandwiches, with pickles and capers.

4. Heavy contact

Poor Des. He had been released the next day and the story died. Bird watching! David brooded on this, falling into one of his silent morose moods, that Sandra feared so much.

'Another crazy trip or is it another woman now? He seems to have lost his whole interest in home, sex, me and Sara. I gave up a great career for him and poor Sara. For what; putting up with his moods? It was that fool Desmond Archer again, that whiz-kid from HMS Eagle, where they were spirited away for months on some weirdo missions that David never talked about. Or was it the girls in the ports. Those really friendly honey-pot girls in Cairo, always out to catch the top business guys, military officers and diplomats; fresh scent, all those silk veils and sparkling eyes... '

She thought, David had never been the same since they edited out the best bits in his naval thriller of the sinking of the Bismarck. She knew David carried a grudge against the aged desk-bound admirals, but had always relished the undercover stuff he had been caught up in those days with the lads from Langley. Was he now off to Budapest and into all that spooks' rubbish, again, when half the world was starving and most of African aid was buried in Swiss bank-accounts?

'David, get real for once', she moaned to herself, as she did the mind-aching ironing, day-dreaming about her log-frame planning tables for the EU and DFID British foreign aid programmes. Scurrying around in Malawi in the Toyota 4x4 Land Cruiser, she had never felt more fulfilled. All that now down the drain, and she going to seed, as she glimpsed in a holiday photo in Greece on the dressing table, the growing pouches under her eyes and her figure sagging. Oops! She singed a silk blouse, her mind full of opaque suspicions, suspect motives and fear of being left alone with her oddly dependent daughter. Her anger fired. 'Oh! Just get lost David with your boring books and fancy women in Budapest!' she shouted to the wall.

The Business lounge was busy, the smorgasbord unappealing to David today. The booming, muffled, flight announcements, as ever, unintelligible, even in the precisely enunciated English at which the Danes were so adept. So small a country, much business was done in English or German, few foreigners ever mastering the local lingo unless they fell in love, in which case their vocabulary was hardly suited to business negotiations.

Then David's thoughts drifted to his old place in that part of Sussex where half the retired Royal Navy admirals seemed to be tending their dahlias. It was a spry seventeenth century timbered thatched cottage, cool in summer and bitter in winter, with its single brick walls which probably, a hundred years ago or more, had replaced the original wattle and daub. Lovely pears in the autumn, damsons and some plummy plums, too many to eat or to bottle, even if he were there again with Sara and Sandra, during the ripening season. Those fleeting moments that give such joy to family life were now spaced farther apart, as he followed this unfathomable course in which he seemed to be sleep-walking.

Was it the aroma of pickled herring and capers that nudged him from his sweet memories or the bulging waist of the heavy who crashed down beside him, reeking of garlic and Dutch gin? David's flight was now marked for departure on the perpetually clicking master-board. He must have dozed. Downing his fruit juice, scoffing some salted nuts, nodding to his overlarge neighbour, he made his way to the gate. Another trip, another anxious arrival, never to be sure when his number would be called and his dreary life transformed into stomach wrenching fear of the unknown, without a safe exit. He was now unremittingly enmeshed. He fished in his pocket for his airline ticket but extracted an unsealed envelope with an address scrawled on it in a wavering hand: 31G Andrassy ut, Budapest. Contact: N. He filched his ticket and passport from the other pocket and was through to boarding as he looked back glimpsing the bulging heavy, sloping off.

5. Budapest

At the Budapest, newly named Ferenc Liszt, airport, not Ferihzy, as David had previously known it, he arrived on time and took a cab to the Three Star Inn Hotel in the centrum, where he had stayed in the past. Down market, stuffy rooms that smelt of the last occupant's take-away and then the dull breakfast; but he would save on expenses paid at the official rate for the country. Its other merit was it was close to the stunning neo-Renaissance Opera house, where he had booked a €74 ticket in advance for Verdi's Otello for the following evening. He found his room, dumped his bags and phoned Sandra on his mobile. She was furious.

'You shit! Sara has had glue ear, probably for years. Nearly deaf with it.' 'Glue ear, what's that.' 'The school doctor found it today. Hold on, I wrote it down somewhere… Yes, Glue Ear: Otitis Media with effusion, whatever that is. The ears get stuffed with liquid that gets consolidated and causes deafness in some cases. Hers was a serious case of it, and made us think it was autism. They'll fix it on Monday at the clinic but seems she'd missed all her school medicals since she was five. Your bloody fault, for all that globetrotting. All those tantrums and reclusion was just deafness. Bloody deafness. When are you back?' She screamed down the phone.

'Look Sandra, darling, I have just arrived in Budapest and I shall probably be back on the flight on Saturday evening. Great news for Sara: we must celebrate together, poor kid she has had a tough time, we thinking she was... you know autistic or something.' There was a click: Sandra had cut him off.

Then a knock, 'Room service.'

David opened the door, no-one there, but a long white envelope on the floor, addressed to him. Inside a curt message, Come tonight at 10pm, N. His contact. It was already 7, so time to unpack, brush up, quick bite at a café and then whatever... He wandered from the hotel at 8.30

to the Muvesz Kavehaz café for a club
'szendvics' and one of their exquisite Esterhazy
cakes, washed down with a chocolate milk-
shake. The atmosphere was of freshly baked
pastries, newly roasted coffee beans and
expensive fragrance worn by elite clients of the
smart set. Then at 9.45, he never liked to be late,
David briskly moved along Andrassy Street, to
check out 31G, the heavy had indicated, to find
out whoever was N.

He pressed the security button and heard
a recorded voice. The door swung open and he
climbed the winding stairs with their automatic
lights that came on in front and off behind as he
progressed. Flats A, B, C; then another flight of
stairs: D, E, F. The door to F opened as he
passed. A young, tall, veiled woman paused,
smiled at him and went on down. Another
flight, he was getting out of breath. At the top –
two doors. One a glass paned fire-exit leading
onto an elegant garden roof terrace: the other
flat G. He rang the bell. A shuffling behind the
door. Someone probably looking through the

peep-hole. Chains being undone, bolts released and the door opened ajar.

'Ah! You! David?'

He smiled, as an elegant, mature woman finally opened the door, kissed him on both cheeks and motioned for him to enter. He sensed a heavy perfume of orange blossom.

'I'm Natasha! Come in. We have to talk.'

He followed her into the lounge overlooking a stunning aerial view of the city. In front, facing the large patio windows was a tall man. David hesitated. He knew the shape. And then as the man turned smiling broadly, David gasped,

'Zac!'

6. Trapped

Zac embraced David with gusto, smelling of garlic and goulash.

'You saw the execution video. Great hoax, huh? The CIA in Langley are doing these as a routine to up the ante! ISIS are just going mad about it. So, I am in a kind of limbo! But we have some new stuff for you with your Arabic from your time in Cairo. I must dash, Natasha will take care of you and explain. You perhaps remember her from Tallinn. She came over to us after the Gorbachev time, when you had left. She told me she remembers you, how can I say, very well!' Zac embraced David again; he kissed the woman on the forehead and then went off, closing the door behind him.

'Drink?'

Natasha smiled.

'Just a fruit juice for me.'

As she prepared drinks in the kitchen area of the enormous open-plan room, David searched his memory about his encounters in Tallinn. He drew a blank. Were they bluffing? She came over to him with the drinks. 'We danced', she said, 'at the consulate cocktail with the navy boys. You must remember me. In those days, how can I say, we KGB girls were not there just for the dancing.'

She spoke languidly with a very slight Russian accent. He guessed she might be in her forties, well preserved and brimming with expectation.

'While you sip that let me explain the mission.'

She invited him to sit on the large deep sofa, and sat beside him, her orange blossom perfume pervading his senses.

'The job we have for you here, with your knowledge of Arabic, is…'

David was feeling drowsy. She asked if he was alright, putting her hand on his thigh. She bent over him, kissing him warmly and then he slipped from the sofa onto the floor. Out, quite out.

He awoke at first light in a soft wide double bed, seeing her asleep beside him. As he stirred, she opened her eyes and kissed him again.

'You haven't done this for a long time, I guess. Don't worry we have plenty of time. I'll brief you over breakfast.' She heated some pastries, made some coffee, poured some more fruit juice at the breakfast counter and settled onto one of the high chairs to chat.

'You see we need your help to screen the refugees. They have been filtering ISIS rebels through these leaky boarders for ages, and now with the Taliban taking Afghanistan, difficult to sort the sheep from the chickens.'

He murmured, 'goats', munched a crisp hot puff fish pastry and sipped the apple juice. He felt unusually drowsy again. As he began losing it, he saw Natasha leave the flat, locking the door. Then a key turned and the veiled tall girl he had passed on the stairway came in, whispering as she came to him,

'Welcome to ISIS.'

He knew then he was being taken, so pretending to be half asleep, he opened his wrist watch mobile and sent of a brief sms to Sandra.

'My wife', he muttered to the girl as he dropped to the floor and felt his hands being tied behind his back and a tape stuck across his mouth. His last thought was,

'Damn! So, I'll miss the Otello tonight.' Yet already winging over the ether to Copenhagen was the last text message he would be able to send for some time.

'Budapest is lovely is booming. Have just got for me breakfast. Call up Desmond next priority for contact. In haste like Holmes.

7. Maryam

'What's this Sara?'

Sandra bellowed, to her daughter who was probably submerged in the attic on digital, puzzles or hacking someone's private social media.

'Can't it wait, Mum. I'm busy?' 'No, it bloody can't. It's your mad negligent globe-trotting Dad, from Budapest. His sms. Double-Dutch to me.'

'Probably one of his codes. Does it mention Holmes?'

'It ends, In haste like Holmes.'

'Hang on, coming down.'

'Here let me see.'

She grabbed the mobile, took one look and cried out,

'OMG, it's ISIS, he's been taken!

'Don't talk such rubbish. Where does he say that!'

'It's a code Mum, from a Sherlock Holmes story. Just read every other word. So, from:

Budapest is lovely is booming. Have just got for me breakfast. Call up Desmond next priority for contact. In haste like Holmes.

'We get',

ISIS have got me. Call Desmond, priority contact, haste Holmes.

'Mum, what's Desmond's number. If it's really ISIS, they're killers.'

'Try Dad's desk drawer. It's that clown bloody Desmond Archer got him into all this cloak and dagger.' Then she mused,

'Back in Lilongwe the avenues of Jacaranda are probably in full bloom. I'm such a fool.'

Sandra collapsed in a soft screaming rage, while Sara quickly found the number and alerted Desmond who immediately dictated a reply.

'Send this back':

Des OK, says Mum. Look cheerful for Aunt Maryam coming after Budapest book-fair. Keep well. Phone school on Monday. Sara. H

'Got it? Repeat to me the hidden message.'

'OK. Now, send it to him; we have his GPS coordinates and can track him if he just keeps that official issue wrist-watch mobile phone open.'

'Who's Maryam?'

'Never mind; he'll be Ok with her behind the lines. If you want him back safe: not a word to anyone.'

Extract from Sara's diary

15 May 20–

Come to think of it, I never really cried about it 'till he was back again. Hope he doesn't think my black depressions are back. It's hard thinking of all that stuff. The real stuff. Not just being whisked off, but the torture that follows. Revenge for what our guys have done to them suppose, under the Shah, in the Middle East under colonial rule; poison gas to keep them in line, extra-judicial killing and what poor starving girls will be forced to do anytime just for a bar of chocolate from the soldiers. Maybe archaeology could be more fun than this crypto stuff at Russell. But it's chill for me for sure. Hey teddy what'yer think? Not on yr phone again. Told you no more than 1 hour a day! That's my ration too.

The next David knew he was being bundled out of a small plane down a short flight of steps into searing heat. A fast car took him off. When they stopped, he was dragged out blindfolded and still bound. He felt sand under his feet as they frog-marched him into a concrete building, throwing him into cell tearing off his mask and restraints.

The cell was bathed by fierce spotlights and crashing electronic sounds hurting his eardrums: the stench was overwhelming as he saw chains hanging from the ceiling, and on the walls dried blood, vomit and on the ground severed body parts. An ISIS torture chamber.

Suddenly three hooded toughs in jack-boots came in wielding thick wooden clubs. They kicked and beat him.

'Convert or die!'

They shouted in Arabic, leaving as dramatically as they had come. He fainted, weeping.

Was it hours or just seconds later that a bearded older man in Arab dress came through the door carrying some bread, cheese and water? David could not tell nor much cared. He was still alive.

'We want you to work for us now, but you must convert first. That's the rule here. You will have two days to think about it and you will be moved to a house, where you can rest. They may try to ransom you. We shall see. Meanwhile peace be upon you. You are lucky not to be mutilated or dead.'

David checked his phone and saw the sms from Sara. He wept on silently, trying not to look at the refuse of victims' lives strewn across the floor smelling putrid and crawling with flies and maggots.

Later that day he was taken to a house. He woke, alone, slumped in an arm chair. He heard a movement behind him, leapt to his feet to defend himself.

'Don't be afraid. Peace be upon you, Dawood. I'm Maryam.'

8. The Imam's blessing

Maryam tended David's wounds from the beating and explained what will now happen to him. She told him she was effectively a slave having been captured in the civil war in Syria after her parents, husband and daughter had been brutally killed by the government forces in front of her. She was abandoned, then caught up in a wave of counter attacks by ISIS, who executed dozens of Assad's militias, and took her and many other young women as slave girls to this camp in Mosul. Her interrogator found she was a teacher, specialising in Islamic studies, so instead of abusing her she was given the job of persuading the most valuable captives to convert and work for ISIS. So long as she was successful, she would continue to be spared the fate of the other slave girls.

'We have but two days. Then if I fail, both you and I will be finished, abused, mutilated, dismembered, or perhaps crucified

59

together, or if we are very lucky simply beheaded.'

'Are you afraid too?'

'Why should I be afraid,' she laughed, 'when I may either be a martyr or receive a thousand blessings for converting you to the faith and gain a place in Paradise!' She lowered her eyes and asked him softly,

'Do you have faith? Are you one of the people of the Book? 'I know you are afraid. That is only reasonable. They like people being afraid of them here. They think that makes them powerful and makes you obey.'

'Beheading would be a blessing rather than the torture they seem to relish here. Clean, quick, final.'

'Remember always, my brother, the good Lord is merciful. You must learn to love him. Fear is not the route to Paradise. The way is by love. First by love of yourself, then of all others, even ISIS, and then ultimately by love of God, the ultimate reality.'

'I have no faith left. What I had, I lost on the way. I fear that death is now very close. I am a lost cause. Leave me to the hooded swordsman.'

David's mind recalled an encounter with a philosophy student at Sussex who suggested a wager on the existence of God. David jokingly replied that's no game, chum: if I win, I win all; losing, I lose not a thing! Now he knew it was for real; his very life was at stake and hers. Was such a God so cynically pitiless?

'Listen I will teach you the basics and then arrange for an Imam to come tomorrow to receive your declaration of faith. Then we will both be blessed.'

After her long sessions of instruction, the next day Maryam told him the Imam would come. Later after their evening prayer together, she lit some incense sticks, with a fragrance of sweet roses. A tall bearded man appeared in Arab dress, enveloped in a dark cloak and with a white cotton keffiyeh headdress secured with a leather agal. He spoke in Arabic to her. She nodded and he asked David for his confession of faith. Then the Imam chanted some prayers and verses from the Koran. Maryam spoke to the Imam again. He looked at her quizzically and mumbled some further words gesturing to David who offered some further words of assent. Then the Imam left, offering a blessing to them both.

Maryam smiled warmly at David and for the first time hugged him close. He withdrew and cautioned her that they must keep their distance. She smiled, lighting some more incense which imbued the room with soft wafts of scented haze.

'Come to me. We are one!' She hugged him again.

'Tis true, I am converted and therefore your brother.'

'Well yes,' she responded, 'but more than that.' She smiled, lowering her eyes. 'You see, the Imam married us. You are my husband!'

'But I am already married.'

'No matter you can have four wives; anyway, non-Muslim marriages do not count. And Desmond tells me you need someone to really love you.'

'Desmond Archer?'

'Yes. We are all working together now, on the inside. But first, come to bed! Don't be afraid. We have the Imam's blessing.'

9. Torture

'If you not co-operate, Maryam goes!'
The ISIS henchman threatened David the next day.
'She sold to Josh, who lusts for her day by day.'
'Take me to your boss,' David said quietly to the tough.
To protect Maryam, David confessed his Allied Intelligence connections and knowledge of the plans against Syria, Russia and ISIS. He was then threatened with brutal torture unless he revealed more details. In desperation he agreed to work for ISIS as a counter-spy. Maryam was allowed to visit him again.
'Don't give in to the torture. If they kill you, you will be a martyr for the true cause and live in Paradise forever.'
'Not sure I'm the martyr type.'
A brutal English ISIS thug dragged David away back to the torture cell.
'I mutilate and then behead all the captives here who refuse to comply.'

He brandished his curved blunt knife and boasted of the score of body parts he had severed. That was his trade mark for those who refused to comply with ISIS demands.

'You must work with us to get ISIS insurgents through into Europe via Budapest, or you die horribly here like the others.'

'Let me talk to your people.'

David was marched off to buy his life for ostensible secrets of the Allies' plot for undermining ISIS through an elaborate diplomatic hoax. He was confronted by a slim Arab, who politely introduced himself as Hussain, dressed from head to toe in white cotton cloth, with an elaborate headdress, carefully manicured hands and nails, with a faint perfume of lily of the valley. He responded to David's colloquial Arabic, in fluent, immaculate, rather academic upper-class English, which he must have refined at Oxford.

David confessed, 'For some years we have been hacking into the Kremlin data-base and have the Russian plans for engaging allies in Syria to fight against ISIS whilst liberating more Russian enclaves in all former Russian countries.'

'Indeed, my good man, yes, we know, all that and more aplenty. We are engaged in hacking too, you know, old boy! Part of the Great Game.'

The allied strategy, David explained, is to maintain instability across Middle East and to infiltrate ISIS, by sending back refugees who have been turned.

This all seemed wildly plausible but it came from a scenario he and his daughter Sara concocted in a diplomatic version of Risk they had been playing.

Hussain, smiled and swallowed the bait and called an assistant to put this all on social media to discredit the Allies, with he added, the most recent sigint revelations about the use of the US Chagos military base in the Indian Ocean, which was now a rendition centre and a store of chemical weapons, banned landmines, barrel bombs and a stock of field-class nuclear warheads.

Hussain turned back to David with a salaam. 'So, David, you will work for us to help bypass security in Hungary and get our Caliphate brothers to make mayhem in the streets of Germany, France, Italy and the UK. Keep Maryam and you will be well blessed. And peace be upon you, brother.'

David was then taken by boat and bus to the coastal region of Croatia and put on a smelly fishing boat full to overflowing with desperate refugees. The next day the boat was picked up by an Italian Navy surveillance vessel and all but a few, who had drowned or succumbed, were landed in southern Italy. They trekked on by bus and train until they reached Hungary where David was swiftly moved on by car arriving in Budapest the next day.

The customs' checks had been rudimentary. At a reception point he was able to shower and change from his Arab dress into the issue trainers and jogging suit provided through the SIRIUS migrant help group. He melted into the crowd of hundreds of other refugees escaping from Kabul and the Middle East maelstrom of war and rapine. He now found himself, exhausted and five kilos lighter than when he was last there, at the door of Inter-text in Oktober ucta, Budapest

It was open. He stepped inside, past the shelves of neatly stacked books with that inevitable aroma of fresh glossy paper, and came to the service counter.

'My name is David Brand. You are expecting me from the Copenhagen office. I was somewhat delayed.'

A middle-aged plump woman spoke.

'We were expecting you last year. Whatever happened?'

He was shown into a back office to find a whole group greeting him with bear hugs and raucous laughter.

'Welcome back, defector! We have some work for you.'

He was back at last with Desmond, Zac, Maryam and hiding her laughter, in the corner, his green haired eccentric daughter, Sara.

'With the defector and the delightful misfit,' declared Maryam, we will make a great team.

The Defector's Daughter

10.   Back to Blighty

Extract from Sara's diary
Wow! He's back. Must tell him all the news.
The ears, Emma and all that maths, books,
museums, modern art, jazz and her odd men
some of them bios difficult to tell. That make
up - and skin tight tights!. Racing through the
exams and free at last.
It'd better be the Che top, the converses, the
distressed ginger jeans and the green wig.
Sandra and her new boyfriend off, off, just
fucked off. That will knock him out and lots of
those bear hugs just for me now. The old
cow. Fed up with Teddy- just no response,
not fully equipped any way.'

'Look I'm not really up to all this, this Kaftan and Armalite stuff anymore. I just need a break. Time to sort myself out' David slumped in a chair, knocking a glass bottle of sparkling water from the office table. It shattered on the marble floor, with a faint scent of almonds.

'Let's repair to the backroom. I'll get the cleaner to sort this out,' Des said. As they moved David, Sara put her arm round him, kissing him softly on the cheek.

'It's OK Dad. OMG, you creeps. Can't you see he's all-in. Dad let's go back home.'

'Copenhagen?'

'No, you lowlife! Sussex. Lower Sheer. Pear Tree Cottage in summer. Our real home. Where you can watch the cricket and have lunch with your navy chums. Where half the retired Royal Navy admirals are tending their dahlias.'

Desmond, David's minder intervened. 'Look David, mate, we desperately need you here. It's vital we stem the flow of terrorists slipping though the net as war refugees. You've got the cover and the Arabic.' David had always thought Des had a tad too much masochism in his character. Des grunted.

'I think Sara's right.' Maryam said very softly, ruffling David's fair hair. 'He's no good to you like this.' She saw David's shoulders heaving as he quietly wept.

Sara was weeping too. 'He's all in, can't you see,' she blurted, covering her face in a crumpled tissue from the pocket of her distressed pink jeans, with rough holes at the knees. 'Can't you see, you bully!' David took her hand and pressed it to his cheek, smiling comfortingly at her and putting his finger to her lips urging her to be less demonstrative. She knelt on the floor and laid her head on his lap. 'Dad, I think I've had enough too...'

'Not sure we can make it safe in Sheer, Des pronounced. It's rather remote in that clearing in the woodland and the surrounding farms and market gardens. What do you think, Zac.'

'It's as good cover as any,' interposed Zac, David's old companion in arms.

David's mind drifted from the bookshop in Budapest to his home in Lower Sheer, with its succulent damsons. He felt trapped in this bookseller scam, frantically wanting to escape it all, the terror, the uncertainty, the pain. His troubled mind turned to more restful times as he gently stroked Sara's head in his lap. David mused on the blossom on the cherry trees in Spring and the swallows swooping over the lawns in the gardens full of linnets, the daisies like a wedding carpet of tossed confetti and the meadow pastures with their bright fulsome buttercups and deep red clover munched by the nonchalant cows; the mellow smell of fresh cut grass, the martins returning to their nests under the eaves, high below the white gables, and the gentle sounds of willow on leather as the cricket season started with the discreet clapping and mutterings of well-played, good shot and the rest of rural England at its best.

And then those lovely country walks with his daughter, her lilting laughter, warm long fingers in his, exploring her quirky mind, so rich and strange and full of extraordinary promise, and the damp leaves under foot with the tangy odour of fox under the hedgerows, the ever-yellowing gorse and the hum of bumblebees in the clover....

Then David jerked back from his daydream into the harsh reality of the present.

He thought of Sandra. 'But Sara where's your mother?'

'Hmm! Some mother. She's gone off with a Chinese business tycoon on a save-the-starving-millions jaunt. Back to her old trade planting safe loos for the third world. Left me in the lurch just before the HSC exams with Aunt .... '

'Emma, your sister. They call her the cranky cryptologist from the British Embassy in Copenhagen?'

'Yeah Emma. Took me under her wing. Some culture vulture. Every museum and gallery, and she's scary too with Gordon that live-in Nigerian basketball player. Says he has a great torso. Could see it bulging in his shorts.'

'Sara! Not now.' David sighed. For Sara was really growing up fast and had been probably initiated into all kinds of stuff with that weirdo Aunt. 'Not the Jazz club as well?

'Yep! That too. Feisty is the word for Emma.' Your late brother-in-law was holding her back. 'Eager Emma now. Much so, after a little pot!'

'Sara, not that!'

'Nope. Just took a sniff and went yellow. Not even into fags, even from Eton!'

It was good, David thought to see Sara liberated from her deaf prison.

'Oh! Yeah. By the way I've been offered a place at Cambridge. Youngest ever, seems! But have to have a chaperone. Statutory rules to protect youngsters from predatory Dons.'

'Cambridge?' David blurted? What's all this? Too young for all that yet.'

'Dad! Trust me, I'll be fine. Just need a chaperone. Want to come?

'But I thought we were to be in Sussex together.' David felt sick, tears welling again in his sunken eyes.

It's OK Dad. Not 'til October. We can be at Pear Tree for at least ten weeks before I go up to Russell College, and I promise to make you some damson trifle, your favourite.'

'Russell,' interjected Desmond. 'That'll be great. Or perhaps awesome, Sara! We have implanted there a kind of son-of-Bletchley Park – cryptology and all.'

'Yep, Emma briefed me and has put in the good word that got me an interview. She was a Fellow at Trinity, told me all the dirt on the new Apostles and the Hardy disciples.'

'That's what happens when I'm away then. He started weeping again'

Maryam pressed David's hand. 'Hold your steeds.'

'It's horses,' I think you want, suggested Sara.

'OK, then hold your horses or even camels! David needs repose. You slave drivers are like the others. Very much.'

'Right,' Desmond concluded decisively. 'Back to Blighty.'

Within the hour David, Sara and Maryam were chauffeured off to the Three Star Inn Hotel, where David found a gift of three tickets for the Marriage of Figaro.

Back at the bookshop, Zac aghast, interposed,

'Bit much, Desmond!'

'The bottle?'

'Cyanide?'

'Can't be too careful when they come back. He's been turned?

'He guessed and smashed the bottle?'

'He's well trained. He'll be checked and debriefed in London.'

'And Maryam?'

'Indeed, and his startling daughter, Sara, she'll' be soundly programmed at Cambridge.'

11.   Make it look like ISIS

*Transcript of audio text at HQ anti-terror
centre London*

'And   Archer', make it look like an ISIS job this
time. Bit of a gaff with the cyanide. Been
reading too much Ben Macintyre!'

'Al Qaida, might be more subversive; If ISIS
turned him. The Empire strikes back.'

'Whatever, Archer, he's been turned. We need
him labelled defector and then wasted. But
make it stick. Totally deniable, of course. And
bury Inter-text. Way beyond its sell-by-date.
Close down Budapest. The birds have flown.
Mosul's cracked open. The Turks are after the
Kurds, the Taliban are on the rampage behind a
veneer of double-talk, so the risk's now here,
everywhere we'll have those sadistic Daesh
brothers-in-arms return to base in Paris,
Washington, sacking tourist beaches, gay night-

clubs, streets, with the suicide vests, but these days mostly lorries, cars, trains, postal bombs.'

"And the girls, Ma'am?'

'No. Not yet. Still our assets. Keep tabs on that juvenile nut case.'

'Sara?'

'Is that it?'

'Yeah, the strange Brand girl, bit of a super star!'

'Russell can deal with her. Who's our bod there?'

'Geoffrey James, Professor of…'

'Yes, yes, Archer. Brief him will you. Now!'

'And by the way get Brand's sister Emma's on the case. Yes, Emma, old mate of mine at LMH.'

'Still on our books?'

'A sleeper. Sound record. Check her out. Not a word about David, though.'

'How?'

'She can bring the juvenile on. Prepare her for Russell. Emma's straight… a bit weird at times. Good cover. Best hacker we're ever likely to have. She has that Nigerian giant Gordon in tow. Class of 2005. They say he's rather well endowed. A real handful!'

'Checked his file last week. Clarabelle's honey trap report, said he was – Hm! A massive challenge, but silent as the grave. Her very words.'

'I need a break, (muddled possibly with a bonk)'

'And, Archer, be sure to have a plan B. I want this sorted. OK.'

'That's all, then Ma'am.'

'I've marked it B/F two weeks.'

'Door opening).

'Archer, don't mess it up again. Two weeks; just two weeks.'

'Timothy, look up short breaks in Guyana for me will you, Timothy dear.'

'Will do, Miss Harcourt.'

Hm, Harcourt thought, maybe transfer him as a staffer. She cast the fantasy as Timothy came in with coffee and a smirk on his face.

'Just printing the details of the Guyana jaunt. That be all, Ma'am?

She nodded, going back to her paper-work, warming to the idea of another clandestine break and maybe even a personal assessment of

that giant Gordon, if he would be quite up for it.
She liked the idea of silent as the grave.

'But...then...trust   no-one...especially   not
yourself.'

12.   Pear tree cottage

Sheer may never have been quite fashionable: Lower Sheer even less; but huddled the length of the hillside, tumbling into the valley with its rippling chalky stream, it remains discreet and with a short trip to the street market in Francisfield it was always manageably cheap to live there for retired naval officers; mercifully, too, for the abiding tastes of sailors, it is within striking distance of Portsmouth, with its bristling pubs, the fleet at anchor in the deep water harbour, sailing clubs, fishing, seafood and the pretty girls they perennially net. Moreover, Sheer continues to boast its market gardens rich in seasonable fare, and beyond, the small farms provide fresh milk, butter, eggs, a variety of fruit, locally treasured from the scattered orchards, homemade cider, and livestock including chickens, turkeys, lamb, deer, goat, ducks and geese, wildfowl, not to mention the occasional farmed rabbit for the pot.

Sheer is forever neatly manicured, nourishing the cottage of the actor Sir Alexander Malt and the celebrated multi-Oscar winning Tarquin Lewis, reared at the local progressive boarding school. It is sedately off the A3 and M3 motorways which cut through north of the area, to London and to the southwest: its peaceful narrow country lanes, with but local traffic, offer the safe and serene occasion for the morning constitutional after the leisurely breakfast, with its struggle with Telegraph or Times crossword, and before the elevenses, which mark the mid-point to luncheon. Breakfast is taken in the sun-lounge or, weather permitting, in the shaded garden with its willows and silver birches; the butterflies and bees bustling softly in the fruit orchard and the cottage garden blooming with hollyhocks, foxgloves, long legged daisies and floribunda roses; then the retired admirals take a leisurely lunch followed by an afternoon nap browsing the latest Spectator or for the livelier minds searching for lampoons of their chums and rivals in Private Eye.

In this serene setting David curled up with Maryam as they dozed, slept, embraced and slept again for three days before he emerged from his shell to play some tennis on the garden lawn with Sara, while Maryam watched under a sun-umbrella and sipped the cooled sherbet and honey drink she had made, keeping an eye from time to time on the kebabs and prawn salad she had prepared for their snacks.

'So, it was four A*s that earned you the place at Cambridge,' David called across the court as he made a sharp drop volley, with Sara still marooned on the base line, from their longest rally. Anticipating this ruse, Sara was on her toes racing to the net and seeing David advancing too, she chipped a lob over his head forcing him to retreat and attempt the clever backhand drive between his legs, with which, once, he had seen Roger Federer surprise Nadal; but David became so tangled with racquet, ball and tennis shoes that he tumbled over on the grass and burst out laughing. Maryam looked up from sipping her sherbet, clapped her hands high in pleasure crying out, 'David, laughter again. Welcome to your new life of peace away from the grips of war. I love you',

'40-15,' announced Sara preparing to serve for the set, as David was still rolling on the grass filling the quiet early summer morning with mirth. He rose took the serve on his backhand and swept a drive passed Sara, '40-30, my dear.' Sara completed the set with an unreturnable ball swinging out beyond David's forehand lunge, 'Game and set to Miss Brand,' she called across the court, adding with her sweetest smile, 'And I love you too Dad… yes four A*s but subject to an interview at Russell next week, I fear.

'So!' David responded, 'After the kebabs and more delicious sherbet it will be a tutorial on how to conduct yourself at a Cambridge grilling… and then Maryam,' he advanced towards her, towelling himself and placing a delicate kiss on her veiled head, 'I do declare it will be high time for another snooze, my darling!'

'But Dad you'll wear yourself out at your age!'

'Nonsense, 'he retorted, 'It's all part of my rehabilitation. Doctor's orders.'

'Which quack was that then?'

'None other than Dr Brand, himself, the notorious sexologist,' he quipped.

'Hey! You're not anticipating an early honorary D.Phil., are you, for just selling all those books in Budapest? I suppose you might qualify if you had actually written them.'

'It's all an essential part of my therapy.'

'And,' Maryam interjected, as she followed them both into the house, 'your therapist will be happy, after our prayers, to offer another hour's delight from two to four, but let's busy ourselves with kebabs and maybe some grape juice I put in the fridge while you were beating your father. He seems to be rather not into the practice of tennis.' 'I think out of practice,' Sara mumbled to herself as she relished the whole transformation her new step-mother was having on her darling father. For he just seemed twenty years younger, under the new therapy. As she set the table for lunch, Sara pondered in her heart how she relished Maryam's understated style and capacity for exuding love, warmth, friendship and compassion, so unlike her own fiercely competitive mother. The day lithely unwound itself to their joy.

Later they went off shopping in the Range Rover to Francisfield, returning with fresh fish, meat and a variety of vegetables unfamiliar to Sara, but which Maryam had spotted in a Lebanese stall in the market and some tasty looking pitta bread, grapes, a sweet-smelling Galea melon, mangoes and dates.

'Stop! Stop both of you. Stay quite still.' They were unloading the car and Sara, with baskets and bags brimming with their purchases was striding to the front door, to open it. David still in the driving seat was screaming out, 'Not another step Sara! He had spotted a brown package on the doorstep about the size of a large but lopsided box of chocolates. 'Stop! For God's sake stop!

The Defector's Daughter

13.   The Robot

It was the strange odour he noted first as he edged forward having leapt from the car easing Sara to the ground. Then David with his trained eyes saw that the parcel was incorrectly addressed to David Brandt. It was sealed with tape but there was no return address and he thought probably an insufficiency of stamps which were not postmarked. Curious: deadly. He had been here before. On the secret weapons' training course in Scotland twenty years ago. David took out his cell phone and called the local police asking for Mike Brennon's number, the explosives expert stationed in Chichester.

They sat in the garden behind the cottage for safety, chatting uneasily about their shopping expedition and the dishes that Maryam promised to cook, including pot roasted lamb with celery and prunes; pastries with honey and Persian chicken with sultanas

89

and ground almonds. Maryam was anxious to get some of the perishables in the fridge, so put them in a shaded place behind a large potted orange tree.

Within the hour, in a heavily protected land cruiser, Special branch SO13 from Counter Terrorism Command arrived, deployed their anti-bomb robot and the crew of four huddled at a safe distance to control its work, filming it as it proceeded to check out the suspect package. In minutes the robot, called Sussex, emitted a short whistle as it had detected explosives. Mary, one of the two senior officers on the crew, checked a manual of devices and sent remote signals to Sussex. The robot withdrew to a safe distance.

Mary ordered all personnel away for the site. The robot, Sussex, ejected a heavy blanket that enveloped the package and then fired on it causing a controlled explosion, which reverberated around the garden, hundreds of birds scattered into the skies, dogs barked from neighbours' gardens, cats squawked and leaves fell from the trees as if autumn had arrived

early in this country village. The house alarms
were triggered and Sara ran into David's arms
as Maryam tried to comfort them both
emboldened as she had been by her experiences
of the viciousness of terrorism. She sighed
quietly, knowing well enough they could never
escape its reach.

The bomb squad departed as quickly as they
had come, robot and all, after they had asked
David to a sign a sheet for their visit and a brief
report.

'Come on Dad, let's go in.

'No wait, wait, not one step further. That may
be just a decoy.'

He took out his mobile phone. 'Desmond, I need
your people. The bomb squad here have just
safely exploded a booby trap parcel device, but
we need a full check made of the premises here
at Pear tree Cottage and the gardens before we
can settle in. The pissing opposition will have
me in the end.' 'Say that all again can you
David, I'm in the loo. Try again in a few
minutes. Booby trap, tell me all about it. Just a
sec.'

David paused a discreet few moments, then his office-issue mobile phone played the Bluebells of Scotland. 'Desmond here. Fire away. Bomb in the garden? David, heard Desmond washing his hands and the bathroom door slammed shut, then the patter of stocking feet going downstairs. David gave a quick summary, robot and all. 'I was really impressed by the local squaddies here.'

'Ah! Yeah! They get plenty of practice with all those touchy retired admirals you have out in Lower Sheer and about. Those prima donna's all think they are prime targets, most of them having been up to something clandestine in their careers. Hush! Hush not a word to their wives and sweethearts.' David mouthed 'And may they never meet!'

'OK then I'll send a clean-up duty crew. Do you have space for a whirly-bird?' Desmond sighed to himself, 'So much for plan B!' 'We do have a tennis court on the lawn at the back. No nets up at the moment. Big enough for a small one about a chain square.' David just loved the old weights and measures and felt rather ill at ease with all the decimal stuff, especially when every Tom-Dick-and Harry retailer had cheated everyone on the conversion. Though one he remembered did not get far with customers trying to sell paint in gallon tins at five shillings and eleven pence three farthings per litre! When the navy helicopter crew arrived, David brought them to the front door and suggested they start their screening there.

'Aye Aye, Sir. Commodore Archer told us to be thorough but unobtrusive, Sir. But it would be wise if you would stay on deck here until we have done a full scan. Don't want another incident. Seems you had a parcel. The local bobbies said all was clear, but you never know with these scumbags from Syria. The local boys in blue told us they found nothing else. But did they look?' 'You're right petty officer. I'll leave you to it.'

Within an hour they had scanned the place, saluted smartly and were on their way saying they had found nothing and all was safe. David went in with Sara and Maryam. He looked around with his sharp counter-espionage training finding three listening devises and a camera that he suspected Desmond's crew had concealed in their scan. He detached them all putting them in his Burberry pocket.

'I'm just off to the local shop get some things we forgot. See you in about half an hour. On his way getting some groceries he called in at the police station to thank them for their earlier help. While there he attached the two listening devises with gobs of chewing gum by the desk sergeant's table and taped the camera in the gent's toilet above a Durex dispenser to the left of the hand drying machine.

'That'll fox the surveillance team analysts and amuse Desmond to know that some of the training I had was worthwhile after all', David ruminated, as he paid the bill at the convenience store and picked up the local paper, smiling at the headline, Cow stuck in sheer canal. Fire service rescue success story, in full, pages 5-7. 'Such serenity!'

Back at the cottage David found Sara, still in shock. He put his arm round her and to take her onto something new, he chatted with her about the format of interviews at Cambridge, as he had spent a year there himself vetting prospective candidates for MI6 before being sent to Copenhagen.

14.   Tobias O Morton

They called him Tom, from his initials. About forty, 72 kilos, wiry, with a crazy Einstein mop of hair, Harris brown tweed jacket, frayed at the cuffs, with green corduroy jeans, gold rimmed round spectacles and always a faint scent of gin and eau-de-cologne which he probably kept in his leather knapsack. He often had his right arm in a lightweight cotton sling, but would release it from his wrist when scribbling on the whiteboard. Tobias had been hired by Emma as a crammer to whizz Sara through the four A levels she had been booked to take in May, loosely attached as she was to Hare College in Sheer.

Sara took to him and to her syllabus with abandon. She was sailing though the Maths and Further Maths and the Cyber security, but kept being diverted in the Physics, becoming rather too engrossed in further exploration of the piezo-electric transducer, LED, and other elements of electronic sensors, and the elements of computer systems' hacking. Tobias, she gathered, was a closet hacker and she wondered whether he had been involved with MI6 as he seemed to have been trawled up by Emma from some distant past connection which neither of them ever talked about, but they clearly had been close, whether as buddies or lovers or both. She always took an antique hat pin she had purloined from Emma's wardrobe drawer of secret treasures, when she had a close encounter with Tobias, who would keep peering at her new lacy bra, not that there was much inside, but his eyes seemed to be attracted by the patterns and the texture. She made a note to talk to Emma about it.

The Autumn turned to Winter turned to Spring. and she seemed to have been holed up almost every hour on her study texts and racing through worked examples and swapping model answers with her new found friends at Hare who made up the 'swots' trio'; along with Sara. The trio included Trixie, a redhead whose magnificent long auburn tresses reached her waist and turned the heads of the young studs; she was the youngest daughter of a navy Vice-Admiral who had started a second family at the age of 50; her real name was Gwendoline, which she hated; and to complete the trio there was Lucy, a fiercely independent feminist activist, daughter of an actor; she had outed Mr Johnson, the deputy head, who seemed to have too much of a thing for young girls; so Sara and Trixie had formed an action group with Lucy, 'Me-three'. Their spokesperson, Lucy, had filed a complaint after just too many close encounters with Johnson's roving hands in the narrow corridors of Hare; indeed, one of their group Chloe claimed she saw a condom, which had dropped on the floor when Johnson in pressing against her blew his nose and whispered to her, 'Well there's a thing young Chloe: if you can't be

97

good, I say, just be careful. And ... why not?' He winked, 'You dear, can come to see me any time in my room. Anytime, you know?

The 'Me three' group has reported him to the young widowed headmistress, Shula Morris, who had asked them to report any further complaints, but they rather suspected she was after Johnson for herself. But they began secretly taking shots on their mobiles of the close encounters and other tricks he had and were already compiling quite a dossier including him rushing to the help of Katya from Poland, who had slipped on the wet floor and he had insisted on massaging her back asking her to undo buttons of her white blouse so he could relieve her distress.

But back to those quadratic equations and the further exploration of backdoors into computer systems, with TOM, who was so vaguely attached to the school on a special free-lance package, like the language assistants from Paris, Moscow and Damascus. 'Me Three' thought it amazing how many of the young lads had taken on French conversation classes when the lovely, elegant blond Beatrice Dupont had arrived that term, replacing Madam Murat who had retired after 35 years at the school.

All 'Me three' did well in the mock exams, Sara sailing through with a full set of A* including the General Paper at AS level. Emma decided it was time to move on. She smiled as Sara told her the detailed results and chatted on about the questions and her responses. She had written about the Great Illusion in her General Paper and Firmani's Theorem in Further Maths. Now they must get down to consider the Cambridge entrance and interview. 'Must get you well prepared for that. Preparing topics and devastating responses. It will be fun, Sara. Never fear. You will just amaze them, never been anyone quite so young and fiery.'

'Like me to help you?'

'Just love it. Wicked stuff!'

15. Sara's boon

Extract from Sara's Diary

12 May 20?? Sheer
*With Dad away. Not knowing what's
happening to him, Emma is a boon, if ever
there was one. Solid! Like she's my sister
and I love it. Wonder if I am going a tad bio,
or what? Love watching her walking around,
swaying her hips and laughing and her
clothes, just a rave. And that scent she uses
from Cairo. Sphinx, I think by a local firm
there that makes it from lilies. Sent Emma an
SMS. Just love time with you: you are a real
boon to which she replied Dear Sara you are
as I was when I was your age, spirited and
tender. Now for the sharpening up. You must
be able to knock 'em sideways at the entrance
exam and interviews. Then Gordon came in
and started gabbling on about his son who I
think of as Gordon II, yet to meet. Said he
was more interested in gym than girls in gym*

slips, is that a thing? Wicked that! And then he flashed his brilliant white teeth. (how do you get them to go that bright? – keep brushing mine – lame.

Emma was in the kitchen, seemingly forgetting that Sara was down.

'How's yer Sporran Gordy? Come let me give it a whirl. 'On my way Ma'am. But we do have a visitor.' 'So just come and give me a hand I'm cooking, sweety Gord!'

He bustled into the kitchen, as Emma had been hiding behind the door, grabbed him and then there was a giggling and something crashed to the floor.

Sara sighed wistfully, as she heard shuffling, the peals of laughter, a rhythmic slithering sound and low masculine grunts and quick sighs, followed by Emma sotto voce. 'Oooh Gordy, tastes divine; quick, pass me some kitchen roll.' 'Let me go first with the tea and cakes, you, hey stand so I can pass... you little raver...'

After a while they both returned with a tray of hot crumpets, little fairy cakes and trifle. Sara noted that Emma's blouse was somewhat dishevelled, her hair awry and a warm glow on her cheeks. Gordon was grinning widely, flashing those teeth and adjusting his sporran, his left elbow gentling nestling against Emma bosom. Both a little out of breath.

'Awesome looking tea, Emma. Hope it has not been too much trouble.'

'A pleasure darling, and Gordon came to help too, so we both were doing it - not any trouble at all. He is such a dear, aren't you a darling. What would I do without you? Emma looked up at him with a sweet smile, pecked him on the cheek and brushed her hand over his sporran.

'Indeed, it's good to see you both in such good spirits.'

Gordon chuckled with a deep resonant sigh. Sara caught the waft of Emma's perfume as he passed her the tray of goodies. Was it lilies of the valley, or that Sphinx she had spoken of, subtle, light and enticing for an afternoon frolic, she had said? How changeable people are. Emma the scintillating intellectual, skewering the greatest academics with well-directed barbs. Sara had seen that at Emma's Cambridge soirées, then the playful lover with her beau, her eyes fixed on his, and their bodies continually close with the lightest of touches, caresses, love taps, in mutual delicate rapture. Sara thought of the young goats in the meadows at Sheer or lightheaded couples in a Shakespeare comedy. Yet there was always that dark side, kept at such moments at bay. The unspoken alertness to danger from the unknown. Evident in the trained reflexes of the combatants they had been, and might be called upon to be again. At any time. They were as sleepers from that world of shadows, skilled in unarmed combat, and adept, if necessary, at slipping a knife into a vital part for a silent kill. That is the reality of keeping the country safe with trained armed and unarmed combat frontliners. All totally deniable when the corpses appear and Inquests find death from assault by person or persons unknown.

Sara had seen the training manuals and talked to Emma about the trade in which she had been an accomplished player; was she somewhat addicted to the action and the perils?

Her life indelibly marked by that secret espionage, as Sara's father, villainy, state terrorism, revenge with no remorse, tranquillity of mind forfeited in continual acts of faith for the cause; that was the market for secrets, a dominant vocation, information, disinformation, and the new fake news, discomfortingly encased within the multi-layered lives and cover lives of the service.

For what? For whom? The answers hidden in a perpetual labyrinth elaborated in turn and turnabout from that little HQ suite of rooms secluded in the offices above Admiralty House. Or, so, Sara believed. The intrigue excited her. The risks, the veiled life where all was an act and no-one could be quite sure who the players were and which side they were on. With no escape. No going back; for they knew too many of the secrets, and were ultimately the keepers of those secrets.

Sara felt herself becoming drawn into being an apprentice in the trade, for which entry into Russell College was the gateway to that life and she relished it in anticipation, despite her father's apparent change of heart that worried Emma. David had warned Sara, wanting to protect her from what he now began to be ashamed of, repetitive duplicity, which cut to his hidden soul.

All three, as they took tea together, knew this, respected and feared it. It was a life of exploration, exploitation, often horrendous, tantalisingly, puzzling; it was like solving a programming error, a crossword at breakfast, with the complexities against a grandmaster at chess: the game of games: lively, lethal as no other. Once hooked, never wanting or indeed able to fold the cards and throw them in.

Sara now began to know she had fallen for Emma, should she go on? Could she stop now? Emma had always been a girl who took the stairs two at a time rather than the escalator; who jumped the amber light before the red appeared; forever bold; who never seemed to grow older; forever feisty, yet so cool. Sara wanted to be like that, but was she getting trapped with no way out? Were they really what they seemed? Or was there a further shadow of deception behind all the playfulness?

16.   David's impasse

David had been looking for an honourable exit, fighting off the withdrawal symptoms that he knew were pressing him more and more as he thought about escape. So far that word was not part of his make-up. Escape? No! But would it come to that. Rather he ached for striking forward; a leap ahead; a full-frontal assault, to capture his future and not remain in the chains of his past; yet his mood swung continually from being becalmed in a sea-going brig or forcing the pace, full steam ahead with the ocean slapping against the bow as the frigate in his younger days would plough through the overarching whitecaps.

David was not fainthearted; just reluctant; not mutinous; merely moodily enduring the game; deprecating this secret life within his brain; the continual deceit; it was the disenchantment that shook him most; the feeling that it had all been a futile fantasy. Who were we supposed to be tricking all the time, with those cruel deceits of trade-craft he was expected to handle? When all the time – such days as might be left to him – he could be happy, tending the dahlias and playing lawn tennis with family and those friends, if he had any left.

Well, he supposed there were always those retired admirals, actors resting, and the brigadiers re-telling their tales of battles gone by or stiffly avoiding such, scurrying around the antique shops for raffish porcelain figurines, their forbearing and no longer sweetly loving wives would secret away in the hall cupboard with a sigh.

Now for those of you readers who thought dissent was unbecoming to a service officer, you should be reminded that a liberal education prizes scepticism as the true foundation of the civilized world. Whilst it is not encouraged, even denigrated in the military services, it survives even there in the principle of trusting no-one in the secret service. And it delves further than that: trust no-one not even yourself; most of all distrust your conscience, if you have any left after the most robust training. Obey commands and do not seek eagerly to take initiatives, except those that may uncover plots and traitors and placate Ministers.

Yet it is clear, David was different. His conscience had survived all brainwashing, in an indestructible response of irritating self-deprecation. It was not so much one that relished sudden bouts of self-humiliation, but rather a cerebral tinnitus, a continual inner voice that denigrated all he did and what he stood for. Like a Shakespearian jester, skipping at his heels, cajoling his every thought and step. David's mien was unlike that lofty distain that some officers displayed seeing their boorish profession as rather beneath their dignity. For David it had been a pitiable burden for himself and for those whom he loved and who loved him; it was a canker eating away the blossom of his life, his chances of joy and of atonement.

For some, they can just get on with the job, without penitence or pity. For David you might wish for the author to free him now. Like an escapologist throwing off the chains. Why not compose a new chapter, like Holmes being miraculously saved from the Reichenbach waterfall in the fatal embrace of the evil villain Moriarty, But why? David is just a throw away character in a thriller. Expendable. No? Yet you might earnestly wish for his expiation. But David knows too well he is lost. A failure beyond redemption, or indeed beyond our hope for his survival at least even as far as the last chapter. David sees his future not in peaceful retirement, for his nightmares resist an inner peace even in sleep. He cynically views his life with pitiless enmity and profound distaste born of sickening guilt, for all the cruelty to others he has caused. The dishonour not even excused by acts of bravery. Mostly he was scared in those awful moments: too scared to stop the brutality, the only way out to save his own skin by more killing of those labelled the enemies of the state, many of whom he guessed were innocent victims, in the heat of the cold war and the never-ending fighting zones invented to keep the arms industry from coups d'états.

David stored in the secret parts of his mind that vision of his youth radiant, full of promise, a player any team would be glad to have as a member. But the dark had come steadily into his life, leading him into the satanic horrors of state crime, war crime, crimes against humanity. After all he had been handsomely paid and assiduously trained in armed and unarmed combat and the handling of those who did his will often against their own people and putting in peril their own families. For what? It was a dissolute, malevolent world. A pit. Yet he was not one to wallow. He saw no way out, but a timely death.

So, should we help him along that path: finish him off, or extend his agony a chapter or so more, until he reaches his inescapable horrific demise? Saving him now would require a rather unseemly coup de téatre, only too common in novelettes. Not quite the done-thing in a post-modern thriller. We could of course employ some extra-terrestrial sci-fi. But wouldn't that be somewhat cheating? I know I am in charge of the narrative, but, I still do have some principles. Now, let us just see what unfolds for our anti-hero, like all those diplomats, carefully groomed and sent abroad to lie for their country.

And yet there was Maryam. She was introduced to offer us the joys of oriental beauty and some hope for the plot. Maryam, David's newest, greatest asset and then he has that wayward daughter the spell-binding Sara to break him off from dire thoughts and bring him back to the comforts of family life... if it were not for the fears of the unknown, the continual fugitive life that was his and threatened to engulf them all. How could he protect them from that? Why should we bother? You might have already alighted from your train, boat or jumbo jet, without having read this far. If not, let's give him some more rope.

He was at a senior office review seminar, with academic eggheads from Denmark, essaying their vision of the world twenty years ahead, with computer-aided simulations, to assess the many forecasts of the likely impact of the expected political, economic, social and religious trends that were now unfolding and their possible purport for defence strategy. His role had been in presenting the underlying factors of the changing world of information, dis-information, defence and commercial espionage and the options for the deployment of these in the coming decades. He had presented a series of travelogues and the scarcely yet explored control of underwater oceanic resources, their significance in defence policy and their threat to ecology.

The strategic value of the environment as a geopolitical military tool is very much on the agenda, especially for small states and those with vulnerable coastal borders. Not since Nelson's time had this been so crucial in terms of national security and the balance of power.

Then, let us leave David to his discourse and turn to more promising matters...

17. Vetting

There was a faint scent of lavender as Sara stepped into the seminar room designated by the College for interviews and disciplinary hearings. The panel detected a rebelliousness in her clothes, the neo-grunge look, short black flared linen skirt, with unevenly cut hem over black ankle boots, various overlapping, short sleeved cotton tops, hanging low, green cropped hair, with dangling beads and a Gothic tattoo on her left upper arm with the inscription Ta Ha!

Sara stumbled as her right foot brushed into a thick double-pile carpet that stretched across two thirds of the room, ending abruptly as it edged into the ornate rosewood pillars of the polished conference table, behind which sat a line of mostly elderly men and one woman, observing dispassionately her immediate embarrassment.

'Good morning, Miss Brand. Do please be seated, if you would' chimed the bald-headed, bespectacled patrician, positioned at the centre of the panel, with the faintest glimmer of a smile, as he rhythmically tapped the fingers of his right hand on the table top, for all the world as if he were signalling in Morse code. She could not be sure but Sara thought the message read in plain language: pretty knees, I'll need a stiff pink gin after this tasty morsel. Yet his suit betrayed his uneasiness, as it was seemingly cut for a broader figure: maybe, she mused, he had shrunk with the cares of office and the relentless slide into impotence.

Before Sara had time to settle herself in the high-backed Chippendale cushioned chair with elegant armrests that he had indicated, from the left side of the group, a crinkly faced woman with a Kashmir shawl and bangles that clattered as she tossed her blue rinsed hair and drawled, 'Impress us!'

Sara wondered if she was expected to do a handsprung and splits or a contralto aria from Verdi's Simon Boccanegra. She turned to the

Kashmir shawl, smiled exposing her newly fitted teeth braces and with a staccato delivery, re-joined, 'Madam, you are looking on the youngest ever candidate for entry to this illustrious establishment. Is that not enough, not merely to impress but even astonish you? However, if you wish I could recite for you Tennyson's Morte d'Arthur or a naughty chapter from D H Lawrence's Lady Chatterley's lover, if the Master would allow me the time! That's my Party Piece.'

Sara had begun by now to fit the faces to the College Staff photo she had studied the day before on the web with her father. Professor Jepson, in the chair, coughed quietly to himself, smiled warmly at Sara's impertinence and uncovered knees, tried to re-establish the momentum for the panel, in which he could see would be the kind of a sizzling session he just loved.

'Tell us Miss Brand, if you would, why you think this College is called Russell College.' He paused with his fingers held upward together as if in contemplative prayer. Sara,

116

moved forward brightly, her youthful left knee now stretched beyond the other, her left hand with its long thin index finger poised to make her incisive response. 'Bertrand Russell, is it not, Lord Russell, Nobel Laureate and all that? Famed for his Principia Mathematica published in 1922 and his latter-day stance against nuclear war in the 1960s, and I believe the youngest ever lecturer in 1896 at LSE, along with H G Wells. Sydney and Beatrice Webb and Bernard Shaw, the Irish Playwright, wit and vegetarian.'

She looked around the circle of faintly amused faces and judged she had engaged the enemy and should thereon in accordance with Clausewitz first principle of battle discard her carefully prepared plan of attack and surf on the initial forward advance.

'So, you have read his Principia?' A grey-haired bespectacled professor on her right interjected. She guessed he was the emeritus professor of econometrics, Krishna Patel from India, a childhood prodigy, who had stormed into print at the age of fifteen with a rejoinder to John Nash on the application of game theory to

East-West nuclear weapons' negotiations and had been rapidly recruited by MI6, being stowed away in Cambridge to keep him out of the clutches of the KGB. She had heard he had a taste for bizarre parties and wore his dyed jet-black hair long to his shoulders and was a disciple of Ramanujan, the village prodigy who had entranced Hardy at Trinity, in the First World War, when Russell was blackballed for pacifism.

'Yes. Of course!'

'So, what did you think, my dear, of Russell's work?'

She immediately hated him for that piece of patronage, and to the chairman's disappointment, tried to cover her knees, beneath the fold of her linen skirt, before firing a frontal assault on her immediate interrogator. She caught him with that two eyed gaze that she knew had the capacity to get her into any movie at half price for a child. 'Well, Professor Patel, I believe...' He looked disconcerted by her gaze and his name being used, as if he was about to be interrogated – an experience from some

118

years ago in Moscow – it was from that he had been left with an indelible wound in his psyche, not that he had been subjected to physical torture, but the psychological electricity of the encounter had burned so into his mind, that he had tried working with an analyst to erase the injury; this had left him with a slight impediment of speech, in which he slurred his consonants; moreover he had developed a compulsive urge to scratch the inside of his right ear, despite his love partner Raj, finding this offensive; this he did now vigorously: the upshot being that Patel now felt profoundly, as he often did at Cambridge, that he was about to meet his match.

'To be precise,' Sara continued, 'I have read his half of it: the half Russell wrote and then the other half attributed to Professor Alfred North Whitehead: true, 'twas a bold attempt at offering a set of axioms from which all mathematical truths could be derived; yet was it not brutally punctured twenty years later by Godel's incompleteness theorem?' Patel moved his head from side to side, the telling Indian version of the nod. Sara elaborated, 'I have to say his Wisdom of the West published in the 1950s was rather more relevant, succinct and inclusive and not spattered with all that obsolete notation.'

Trying to recover some lost ground, Patel unrelentingly continued digging the hole he had started, beads of perspiration, glistening around his aquiline nose. 'When did you read that, then?'

'When I was about eight and a half, in Copenhagen, sitting in the Tivoli gardens in the queue for a Sex Pistols gig,' Sara retorted with relish. 'My grandfather had won it as a school prize.'

'And what did you think of it then?' Patel kept digging, whilst the chairman, looked ostentatiously at his fob watch, which he deftly opened with a sharp click, as he drew it languidly from his waistcoat pocket. 'The John Piper illustrations were too passé for me, more into Kit Barker and Jackson Pollock at the time, but it did get me started on thinking about how to write for people rather than just other eggheads.'

The chairman interjected adroitly signally to Patel to desist, "So Russell, our College Patron, was an egghead in your view?' Sara urged herself on, not to be browbeaten, by this bunch of brainboxes, as she judged they wanted her more than she needed them, it was a buyers' market for her, and she cruised on. 'Indeed, he was, more egghead than A J Ayer, even though he was sacked by Trinity and sent to jail on various occasions, for his social and political views, he just had no street cred and became in his dotage a captive of the nuclear disarmament camp.'

Sara felt she was really flying now. 'My grandfather, who was I suppose an old-fashioned Liberal, would have been a Whig had that party survived, told me he watched Russell lead a CND rally in Whitehall in the 1960's. He had been friends with Russell during the fifties. He said that Russell, who was patricianly leading the crowd, pottered up to the great rosewood front door of the Foreign Office. He was handed, by his chief minion, a large hammer, a nail and an inscribed protest note on vellum, to fix to the door. As he raised the hammer, like Luther, to strike a nail of protest on Foreign Office door, broadly smiling to the cameras as they were clicking all round to capture the iconic moment, the door opened. A discreet civil servant in pinstripes appeared holding out a small roll of Sellotape, evidently appealing to Lord Russell to spare the beautiful door from his intended assault.

Grandfather said, the two courteously exchanged views on the matter and Russell handed back the hammer and nails and to the dismay of his followers, proceeded with some cack-handedness, and with some modest help from the pinstripes, to apply the protest note to the door with the office adhesive roll, sparing the antique door, yet utterly defeating the entire heroic symbolism of the event. The cameras ceased clicking and the crowd melted away in sheer embarrassment, my father recounted. A sad epitaph for a national treasure.'

18. Lured

The panel fidgeted in their Chippendale ribbon backed chairs with their Bordeaux red woollen seat coverings, getting rather frayed at the edges, the faint sweet aroma from the awaiting carafe of port wine on the sideboard wafting through the air. Then a quick intervention from the far right of the boardroom table, as a shaft of morning light flickered through the brocade half drawn curtains, 'Are you a terrorist?'

The question was fired by a round-faced plump man in clerical dress. 'Must be the chaplain', Sara presumed. 'More an iconoclast,' Sara added with a wry grin, 'you know like Jesus in the Temple, chasing away the money lenders, or the Holy Prophet, Mahomed, cracking open the idols in the Kaaba, or Henry VIII demoting the Pope to the Bishop of Rome and the Society of Friends getting rid of priests, chaplains and ministers.' 'So, you're an atheist, then, the chaplain retorted triumphantly.'

'Not exactly, she demurred. 'I rather follow the line of Lord Russell, a humanist, but I am intrigued now, looking into Islam.' This brought whispering amongst the panel, broken up by the Chairman nodding to his left at about eleven o'clock, whereupon a spritely younger-looking academic, whom Sara judged to be the newly appointed chair in communication studies, aka cryptology, tried to widen the discussion by asking, 'What is the greatest novel you have ever read?' Sara had the premonition they were now entering the end-game in this strange encounter, and determined to fly even higher, with adrenaline coursing through her fragile frame, she responded 'I do not consider the novel, as a feeble sub-species of literature, merits the epithet of greatness. Novels are the last recourse of the muddle headed, lacking the discipline to explore the great truths of life and science. Why should one bother to read any of them, finding out how the storytellers think we should lead our lives or avoid the pitfalls of family disasters, and resolve a wide variety of life's moral dilemmas, when history, biography, science and the much-neglected documentation in the National Archive or the British Museum, hold so much more value for the enquiring mind? Novels indeed!'

The youthful inquisitor not to be baulked with this sparkling spontaneous rejoinder to his question, continued, 'So, tell us then, what is the greatest non-fiction you have been reading, in your jaunts to Kew and to Bloomsbury, maybe?' Sara paused wanting to end with another off-beat note to ensure the panel remembered her from all the other candidates they must be grilling, 'Well Professor Geoffrey James, is it I believe?' He nodded. 'Yes, well, apart from Russell and Whitehead of course – I should add in parenthesis, if I may, that I have been working on a rather simpler form of notation for a new edition of their treatise – that apart and of course there is WikiLeaks, I do have a soft spot for R V Jones Most Secret War, Solly Zuckerman's from Apes to Warlords, Hogben's Maths for the Millions, Nassim Nicholas Taleb's

The Black Swan, and of course the Holy Koran, my father gave me for my last birthday.'

She paused, watching the open lipped scrutiny from James. 'But for me, the test of a great book, is not in the elegance of the prose or the depth of characterisation, but whether it is accessible and helpful to the reader in extending their knowledge of life and its purpose. Fiction ain't for me, though I did find D H Lawrence an eye-opener for a young girl.' 'Moreover, if I may,' she elaborated remembering her father's point on 19th century history, I was rather taken last year when I discovered Professor Gareth Butterworth's, masterly work on 19th century history, The Rape of the America and Africa, published by Routledge and Keegan Paul: it's a post-modernist review of western colonialism in brutal unremitting detail, and worth all those fat 19th century three volume novels lined up end to end. It tells us the unexpurgated story of man's inhumanity to man and to most of the native women to boot: it captures the essence of European hubris at its most contemptible, and with extracts from personal diaries of the victims and local contemporary art, it exposes the heartless genocide and destruction of other vibrant cultures that had lasted thousands of years. She glanced across at Butterworth at 3.15, who had been silent throughout: he was quietly beaming and nodded to her.

There was a long silence. Then the Chaplain intervened. 'Of course, we gave them the greatest gifts of all, the Bible and the prayer book for their enlightenment and ultimate salvation through faith... and of course good works. Not a bad deal when all is said and done.' Some of the panel audibly chortled; others lowered their eyes hardly believing what they had heard: Sara smiled sweetly, looking the Chaplain straight between the eyes, 'Rape, is rape would you not agree, your reverend – even as foreplay for endowing the victims with the sacraments.' Had she gone too far? Then she was rescued by the woman with the bangles and shawl, who enquired in a somewhat motherly tone, 'How would you manage here at Cambridge, being so very young?'

Sara came back chirpily, 'Well if you think I look too young to cope, my step mother has offered to be my cook, housekeeper and my chaperone.'

'Chaperone? Exclaimed the lady in the shawl.

'You know, Ma'am' Sara continued, 'one can never be too careful these days especially with the young dons, or, I am told, even some of the rest, encountering their mid-life crisis, men or women. There's much prudence in a chaperone, and mine has promised to take me out to tea if I teach her about computers: amazing how little that generation knows about them.'

The Board room was filled with gentle laughter and subdued chattering. The chaplain having recovered his demeanour and rather liking the iconoclasm in such as fragile frame, slapped his thigh and cried sotto voce, 'bravo!' 'Brava!' corrected the chairman quietly to himself. 'Thank you, Miss Brand,' as he signalled by standing up in front of the life-sized portrait of Lord Russell, by Graham Sutherland, to close the session. 'We shall let you know our views, of course, but I can say now that your written paper yesterday, ahhm, was exceptional and your session today, ahhm,' clearing his throat again, and trying not to gawp at her knees or her green hair, 'a stimulating and charming revelation.'

Sara stood too, smiled politely, nodded to the chairman and each member of the panel, thinking she had really had them for breakfast. But they were not quite done. Professor James shot a googly at her. So, what do you think of the number 1729? 'Aha. The taxi cabs again. Not boring at all, I believe Ramanujam retorted to Hardy, from his sick bed in Putney. It is a very interesting number; it is the smallest number expressible as the sum of two cubes in two different ways.

'And which are? James brightened with some incredulity. 'My God, she has been well prepared,' he whispered to himself. 'The two different ways are: $1^3+12^3 = 9^3+10^3 =1729$! I believe that is right, with the rather cute number one cubed to make up the first count?'

It was over. The chairman beamed and nodded. She rose leaving the panel somewhat open mouthed, and walked steadily to the door, across the deep piled carpet. As she passed into the corridor beyond, she felt the light hand on her shoulder, which her father had told her to expect. It was a young Professor James, the cryptologist, who had spoken in the interview and put that last wicked poser. He was smiling and unnervingly tall, as some are when they unwind themselves from a sitting position, with more height in their legs than torso. 'This is my card and London address. Come with your father and your chaperone if you wish, to join us on Saturday evening: we are having a little cocktail and there are some people I would like you to meet. We also have something to ask you to do. Best keep this to ourselves, Hm?' He smiled warmly and disappeared as quietly as he had come.

Before we move on, it would be right for you to ask how can it be that Sara so confined before, so comfortless for so long, could have emerged that morning, like lightening at the close of a hot summer's day. How could a girl of just so young outshine and confound this

130

arrogant array of scholarly dons: and, alone. But, you see, she is a just sensational child prodigy. You might have asked how did Mozart suddenly hit the European musical scene as a composer and brilliant performer at the age of four; or in chess, or in politics, or in mathematics. She is not alone as a female child prodigy. There was Joana Inex de la Cruz a child Mexican poet and dramatist, Judith Polgar a Hungarian child chess master and Jennifer Pike a child violinist and top international competition prize winner. So, just believe in Sara, there she is and she is not going away for a few chapters yet. So, enjoy the ride.

19.   The Mosque

Now that Sara was starting at Russell College, David, not wanting to be away from Maryam, moved with them both to Cambridge, as support for Sara. Unconventionally she was allowed to live out with them rather than take a room in the College, but she was expected to dine at the college at least twice a week to absorb the culture and make friends, occasionally being invited to sit at High Table, meeting some of the formidable intellectuals of the day and rubbing shoulders with the higher echelons of the security spooks. At weekends David drove them all back to Lower Sheer where they relaxed in a sublime rural retreat.

After a week of settling Sara in and finding the key points for their comfort, they become regulars at Tesco super store with its halal section, the hairdressers and barbers, the book shops, the DVD store, the best bakers, the library and patisserie, take-away restaurants, for

132

modal clothing Habitat, Greenisland, Crazy Girl. David started attending the Mosque for most of the five prayers. Sometimes he skipped Isha, praying en famille at their flat which had a study prayer room. It had writing desks for both David and Sara, a chaise longue and prayer mats in cupboards below the long book shelves, which David had had a local cabinet maker knock-up before they moved in.

David loved his books, though they were not laid out in any special order, as he enjoyed browsing hoping to stir the memories of a good read from years past. He generally had three books on the go. Biographies and histories were his favourites, though he often wondered if the real history of the world was really driven by the stories of heroes and heroines or was more a muddle-through by ordinary people who needed to have legends to admire as models of their better selves.

Soon in the mosque he was on nodding acquaintance with many young and old figures in caps and Asian style gowns, often wearing sandals in the most inclement weather. One

133

evening after the Maghrib prayer, a young Turkish student, named Iqbal, from Sydney Sussex College, introduced himself and invited David to join a small discussion group who were concerned with Middle-Eastern affairs. Iqbal had picked up that David was familiar with Arabic and chatted with him about his own history studies and that he was hoping to do a thesis on the collapse of the Ottoman Empire and the impact on Middle-Eastern trade.

The Mosque itself, then, was ironically a converted Methodist chapel, in which one of the two vestry rooms were used by the Imam as an office and the other as a small seminar room for discussion groups and for tuition classes for the attached Madrassa. This was before the splendid new Mosque with its eco-friendly design was constructed with Arab money. It was in the old chapel that David was guided by Iqbal who introduced him to three other students, one, Imran, a post graduate student from Pakistan studying Persian History at King's, Ismail a young fellow from Syria who was at Madingly Hall, a post graduate Institute of education, and finally Abdulla from Egypt an older mature student at Selwyn who was engaged as a tutor in Islamic studies.

Abdulla talked expertly about new developments in Islam harking back to the classic period of the importance of Sharia law in a time of the early Caliphs and the continual existential threats to the core body of Islam from confederations of polytheists, pagans, the Roman and Greek religious groups, jews, Christians and other monotheistic sects and from those Muslims who just wanted a quiet life and declined to engage in warfare even to defend themselves. Abdulla spoke of Abu Bakr al Baghdadi and the revival of traditional Islamic culture. Some aspects of this revival might seem barbaric, but so was computer guided rockets that the West used with horrendous collateral damage. He sympathised with the rigour of the new style getting back to the simplicity of the origins of Islam in Meccah and Medina, wearing cool Arab style dress, the rejection of alcohol and all that was not strictly halal. The new wave even returned to forms of government by the elders and the refusal to take part in western style elections. Those who wanted to be free- riders, taking the benefits of security and the Islamic welfare state. had to be excluded unless they paid their taxes. Christians could be tolerated on those terms, but girls should convert first before marrying a Muslim.

Ismail interjected as he was uneasy about slavery and concubines. And, surely crucifixion was outdated. Iqbal waxed lyrical on the purity of Sharia law, in which many of the aspects most reviled by western liberals had been part of the criminal laws of many countries until quite recently. Some were even today continuing with capital punishments by hanging and the electric chair and lethal injections, even if they had given up the vile practices of burning at the stake and hanging drawing and quartering. Besides, he argued concubinage saved many women resistant to conversion from death, as did slavery which provided all-found residential employment rather than abject poverty and beggary. Islam was a wide tent. ISIS for example proudly provided free housing, food and clothing for the faithful: a model welfare state. Many of the world's oppressed flocked to join and to fight for such a faith. Those wanting a more peaceful way of Islam could join the turn to Salfiists and a life of continual prayer and Koranic study.

David listening quietly, was guarded as ever in his conversation suspecting that he was falling into a well-laid trap that would soon lead to a tragic conclusion. As the conversation meandered on with no-one seemingly in the lead role, Imran suddenly produced five tickets for the opening match of the Indian touring side at Lord's against the MCC.

'Shall we go like we did last year for the West Indies. I can get hold of my dad's white van. It should be fun. They say Sachin will be there signing bats in the bookshop. You in too David, like cricket?'

'I've played at Fenner's, for the navy against the University. Rained on us, when we should have rolled them over. A disappointing draw. But what a ground!'   David never guessed what was in store and for a moment forgot the old maxim trust no-one, least of all yourself.

20. The young bloods

David liked the group which he thought of as the young bloods, but which was more formally called the Jumah group as they met after the Jumah Friday prayers, when black Turkish coffee was served and Iqbal would often bring baklava honey cakes that his wife Aisha had made. On this day David brought some vegetarian roti and samosas that Maryam had prepared and put in a thermos flask to keep them hot. Imran was delighted. 'Even better than my Mum's at home and the pimento is oooh! Give me water, Iqbal, Wow!!'

'How's your Ottoman Empire thesis coming on,' David quizzed Igbal, whose mouth was so stuffed with baklava and coffee that he nearly choked and Ismail had to hit him on the back before he could recover his breath.

'You know Istanbul and the Bosporus?
'Yep. You bet! Oh! That wistful nostalgia in Orhan Pamuk's writing on the Turkish hüzün.

'The lost grandeur of the Sultans!'

'The Sultan Ahmet mosque; now that's really something.'

'Uplifting. Alhamdulilla!'

'The Ydukuli fortress!'

'The Valens viaduct.'

'The baklava.'

'The Turkish baths and massage!'

'The elegance of the Taksin square and the silent running tramways.'

'Just like in Manchester!

'The Tokapi museum and the treasures rescued from the impossible Wahabis in Makkah.'

'To say nothing of the great staff of Moses, the well blessed. Though when I saw it, sadly it did not transform into that snake that spooked the Pharaoh.'

'And the mint tea.'

'Ah! Indeed, the mint tea, and the baklava, the baklava. Do have another!'

'The Falafel! Chirped Iqbal.

'The Shish kabob, mmmh! Oh! that Adenah kabob too, melts on the tongue.'

David liked this group. He smiled with Abdullah as they all laughed and chatted about their travel stories and the best food in the Arab world around the Mediterranean, and from Cairo to Karachi and Rawalpindi in the Punjab, from where Imran's family had come before settling in Bradford, taking over a woollen factory producing fine Kashmir cloth for Saville Row tailors.

Ismail the tall light skinned Syrian slapped his thigh and in an American drawl beaming like Bush intoned, 'Istanbul! Been there, got the postcards and the porcelain place mats and see my Gallipoli T shirt!' He feigned strutting like Bush, the Texan evangelical. They all chanted in unison,

'Awesome, Ismail. Now let's have your Trump!'

It was his best party piece, smoothing his hair over his brow, pouting and wagging one finger, 'Ah! Those shithole countries! Don't let them in.' He mimed pressing a big button on the table in front of him. 'Poooof! They're gone. Great toy this button, so much bigger than the Rocket-man's! Now for that wall. But let's get

Iran to pay for it. One of the new sanctions I dreamed up last night. Genius smart and sazzy!' They all fell about laughing at Ismail's charade.

Then Igbal nudged Imran who had remained rather aloof. He looked up with a strange fierce glint in his eyes. He raised one hand above his head. A sudden silence! No-one spoke. They just bowed their heads

'Here's to the Jumah Group, and....' Imran looked at each one in turn. 'May we all be faithful to the cause of the Holy Prophet, peace be upon him and his family, and ... I pray we shall all follow in his footsteps and those of the four rightly guided Caliphs. You know our mission.' He added a prayer in Arabic and blessed his companions, who all intoned a long Amin, along with David, rather taken with the occasion.

Abdulla was quite overcome, with tears flowing down his cheeks.

'Before our great mission to Lord's, where, as an Egyptian, I have no knowledge of the game and hope to be there with you in our pilgrimage, I propose... subject to your assent...'

142

'Come out with it, Abi...

'Yeeh! This is not a parliamentary session!' Iqbal interjected still musing on the Turkish hüzün and handing round some Turkish delight, with the powdery icing sugar floating in the air.

'Yeeh! Come on Abi, out with it. I have to be back for my class at three, moaned Abdulla.

'I propose we vote David as our leader in our great assignments.'

'All in favour say Aye,' Iqbal added in quasi-Parliamentary form.'

'Aye, Aye, Aye, Aye.'

David was quite touched by the comradery that had sought to give him this blessing.

'I am overwhelmed. It will be an honour to be your pasha!'

The meeting broke up with warm embraces and a reminder to be ready by the Mosque on Thursday next at 8.30 for the minibus to Lord's.

'And don't forget your tickets!'

As David was leaving, he spotted a mobile left on the floor where they had all been sitting. There was an unanswered message. Curiosity got the better of his discretion. It was marked from MO. He'd seen that somewhere before. The odd message: *Let Brooks try, with spin.* Some sort of code. Then he had a strange premonition, not about the message but the number it was from. He knew that number, somewhere in the back of his mind. Lost it. A sign of the ageing process already upon him. He hurried after the group who were scattered along the road.

'Imran! Your mobile? No?'

Imran frowned, took the phone. Saw there was a message. Clicked. He looked at David uneasily.

'Thanks, brother. Lost without this.'

David nearly had it. That number. He could only think of Otello! A substitution-code? But who was MO. Was Brooks in the England team? A spin bowler?

21. The Soirée

They were heading for elegant flat off High Street Kensington, a stone's throw from the Natural History Museum, where David had taken Sara once, when she was eight, to see the butterfly tent. It had amused them both to have so many highly coloured species alight on their shoulders, their heads and arms as they wandered through the little covered garden which also had an extraordinary collection of spiders. Sara had preferred the butterflies. She had persuaded David to buy a set of butterfly placemats which were still in one of the unpacked boxes from Copenhagen.

They were greeted at an open door by an official usher who checked their invitation cards, which they had downloaded a few days before, and showed them into the main packed reception room where Professor Geoffrey James greeted Sara warmly, mouthing, 'So glad you have come,' above the hubbub, of giggling, droning, chirping, questioning, insinuating, languid and bombastic voices. Sara responded, 'Professor James may I introduce my father, Commander David Brand.' As an afterthought she added for explanation, 'Royal Navy.'

Professor James wrinkled his brow and smiled, 'Yes, we have met, I believe, at Dartmouth, when you delivered that, may I say, rather brilliant lecture on, Post Bletchley Decryption Techniques.'

'A pot-boiler, really,' David, interjected quietly, with his usual diffidence on professional matters.

'But Commander, you were the star, with everyone mesmerised by your analysis of just how insecure are communications in the age of super surveillance, and then of course the wild chit-chat of your exploits in the field. Something akin to hero worship by the cadets I seem to recall.'

'Hm!' David responded wanly, 'All that talk, much exaggerated. Fieldwork's mostly boring, you know, and a handler worse, waiting around for something or someone to turn-up. I joined

146

the navy to see the world and what did I see, mostly the back alleys of foreign ports, grimy offices and endless diplomatic parties.' David added looking down to Sara whose arm was linked with his, 'It's all changing so much, one so quickly gets out of touch.'

'Indeed, Commander, that is the very line of thought that prompted us to take on Sara at Russell and tonight to introduce her, as it were on the crest of the new wave, to some of the people here, old hands and new.'

'So that's what I'm here for,' Sara, interposed, 'A guinea pig!'

'More, a fresh candle to light the way ahead, Miss Brand. So, let's get on and make some introductions to get you started. Do you mind Commander, if I rather monopolise your daughter for a while?' 'By all means, throw her in the deep end. Never likes it better, these days.' 'So, we discovered, at the interview at Russell. Quite knocked us all for six!'

Geoffrey, beamed at Sara and she smiled back at him, looking into his clear blue eyes, with a tinge of green about them, wondering if he now used tinted contact lenses.

'So, without more ado, may I say, Commander and Miss Brand, you are most welcome to this evening, which incidentally includes the launch of a new book by the distinguished military historian, Sir Max Bayeaux, with his sensational sceptical masterpiece, Secret Agents, curse or cure. He will be doing a book signing in the study beyond the band.'

Geoffrey motioned towards the far end of the room which was becoming increasingly boisterous, as the band took their places, tuned up and opened with a selection of numbers from the new hit musical at Drury Lane, Robots in clover.' David released Sara's hand from his arm, as he caught sight of his gorgeous sister Emma, holding court as ever with the diplomats from a clutch of embassies, who were eyeing her flaunted bosoms and responding flirtingly to her light repartee. Sara gave David a nudge and a wink as she was whisked away into the bustling throng of academics, writers, senior embassy staff, documentary film makers, top

148

service personnel and old hands, with whom David had had many a close shave in the field and wore the scars engraved in his heart and some still on the secluded parts of his body.

David smiled back as he saw Sara being guided by Geoffrey towards the distinguished BBC security correspondent and war hero, Frank Trueman. David was immensely confident about Sara in any company even the most challenging: but this was just light entertainment. He knew she was so well prepared for any type of such encounter. She had a rapier tongue, bold in her reactions, but was now developing charm and wit and an engaging manner to conceal that razor edged under-text in her chatter.

David mused that he hadn't seen the need, yet, to pass on to her his official issue encrypted smart phone and his Avon Taser 7 or his Streetwise cell phone stun gun with its 12 million-volt punch, nestling in the inside pocket of his jacket; nor had offered her his TBOTECH 18gram mace spray he carried on his key ring. Her best defence was the advance course in

149

judo he had signed her up for, and she had been so enjoying, in the welcome sojourn they had spent in Sheer that summer, give or take a few problems with the other side. He had also primed her, when in doubt, just ask the question, 'So what have you been up to this year?' and no-one at parties like this would miss the opportunity of swanking about what they had been doing, whom they knew and what countries they had worked in. Most of it false: all of it fun.

Yet what was Geoffrey really up to. Not part of the briefing that David had checked last night on his 6G smart-phone, but he had slipped into Geoffrey's side-pocket a bug linked to a recording device he could down-load later. David sipped his drink and scoffed a well filled prawn spring-roll with what he detected were Thai spices, and squirmed his way thought the bustling throng towards his ebullient sister in full flow, with her satin plunging neckline gown and bare feet. Not the first time she had kicked off her six-inch heels at a reception and had to repair home without them, having lost them pushed under some table or picked up as souvenirs. Emma had many admirers.

'Sara Brand, let me introduce you to my good friend Frank Trueman, famed on the BBC; their security correspondent. Trueman, this is Sara Brand, one of the youngest ever new recruits at Russell.' Sara looked down to see a suave sun-tanned gentleman in a motorised wheel chair, opening the encounter with, 'It's great to see you here, if I may use the phrase, in the flesh, rather than on the box.' He smiled warmly. 'And your new thriller, Deadline, is a real page turner. Love it. Don't tell me the denouement; I'm still on page 336!'

'Aha! Not sure I could tell you the end, I'm so engrossed in writing the next two. But, always a pleasure to meet a reader; can't manage without them...But do tell me Miss...

'Sara Brand!'

"Yes of course, Sara. Forgive me I was rather taken up with your hair colour. Is it real?'

'Tra la la!' and Sara flung off her green wig to reveal beneath a shock of green hair! She peeled into her infectious giggle. Trueman could hardly suppress a chuckle himself though that was not his usual style. He pondered on this for a second and realised he was rather taken with this new will o' the wisp.

'Tell me Sara, do you like happy endings, as I am wrestling with the last few pages of my next book, Mirage.'

'Well, I don't like endings at all you know. They are just false, not like life. Why not finish with a muddle in the middle, like life, a riddle, a cliff edge. Keep the suspense going. Like Scheherazade, or just leave the hero in limbo, hm, make the cut as the heroine is facing the firing squad, or her get-away car runs out of petrol. Now that would please the post-modernists: no end at all. What was it David Lodge said about novels and reality...Literature is mostly about having sex and not much about having children: life is the other way round!'

Trueman looked at her again. 'My dear Sara, I'm just sorry we have not met before. You've just given me about half a dozen fresh ideas and we haven't even danced!'

Oh, it's nothing really: I often come up with half a dozen original ideas before my cornflakes,' Sara chortled, 'She added flightily, my dance card is not entirely taken up, I am sure I can fit you in somewhere, how about the salsa?'

'Hmm! I might have to sit that one out, he giggled.'

'Come on Mr Trueman, I can whoosh you round in this thing, if you show me the right buttons to press.' Trueman had not had such a good time for years. He laughed and laughed at this slip of a girl taking him on at his own game.

'Sara, hold on a tad. Hold on. Let's take it more sedately. This is not a student rag ball you know.'

'Yeeah, but what fun, the salsa on wheels!'

'Now Sara, you are starting very young I hear, so what field are you going to specialise in, have you thought about that.'

Sara frowned. 'Is he just an old fogey like all the rest?'

Frank Trueman, though, was no fogey. If they celebrated today heroes as in Ancient Greece, he would be in the great Pantheon. He came from a modest family background, his father a mason living in the suburbs of London. Frank was an unexpected arrival, he thought probably a burst condom the cause, when his mother was 49 and said she was experiencing the change of life. The earlier children were then all grown up and out at work. Frank was nurtured with enormous affection. He won a scholarship to Latymer Upper School Hammersmith doing modern languages, including Russian and Arabic and oddly economics. From there he progressed to Balliol College Oxford, reading PPE, gaining both a double first and a blue in cricket. He was recruited by the BBC as a correspondent in Moscow and then in Washington following Charles Wheeler, whom he greatly admired as a journalists' journalist. Whilst with the BBC, he was approached by MI6 to provide background briefings on political and social change. When the BBC assigned him to do some work on the Colombian drug cartels, he also clandestinely gathered intelligence, reporting it back to GCHQ. During one of his sorties to interview a drug baron, he was ambushed, shot multiple times and left for dead. Happily, a passing ambulance took him to the nearest hospital where he remarkably recovered, though paralysed from the waist down and confined to a wheelchair. After a long-term rehabilitation he returned to the BBC and his links with the Intelligence services. He continued his interest in sports competing in archery and pistol events, with evident superior skill despite his disability. He was no fogey as Sara was yet to discover.

David sidled up to his younger sister Emma, kissing her cheek and pinching her bottom.

'Hey! None of that!' She turned to slap his face and fell about chortling. 'David, Dearest David it could only be you, but for a moment my heart missed a beat.'

'In shock or was that hope, Kid?

'Oooh! You rascal, David! Come on do it again!'

They embraced and whispered old stories from their childhood memories, playing in the warm willowy grass, discovering, toads, the charms of magic mushrooms, the arrival of the ardent ram and then the lambs frisking in the weak February sunshine, the daffodils and the bluebells in the meadow with cowslips, chest-high wild daisies and skinny dipping in the river in those far-off hot summer evenings which never seemed to end with the sun not setting until after mother's bedtime call across the verdant fields.

'Well apart from playing tricks on all those old hush-hush field staff, I'm into cryptology and AI,' Sara continued, trying various buttons on Trueman's chair. Better than boring scrabble!

'Hey! Hey! Not the red one: that's my ejector seat.'

'And the blue?'

'That's the flush loo when I get caught short.'

'And this green one decorated with a fleur de lys?

'Keep my tablets in there.'

'Sedation?'

'No! Viagra!'

'Oooh, what's that for? For fun, or illegal! But…
she felt out of her depth and a little uneasy. Bye!
I think I should circulate a bit.'

'Hm! Come back later,' he mused to himself.
'Little sylph. Steady as she goes.'

David turned to his left and found a
familiar face close to his shoulder. 'It's John
Square, I believe?'

'No Bernard O'Flaherty, the Tempsford man?'

'Indeed.'

'Make it larger print next time. We old hands
have to use magnifying glasses as it is. Makes us
feel a bit like Sherlock Holmes, minus the curly
pipe to say nothing of the hypodermic syringe
for the cocaine addiction.'

'Never knew how Conan Doyle got away with
that with his publishers at the Strand magazine;
those days they just went along with that.'

'Interesting history under the editor H G Smith,
who had a galaxy of stellar writers in tow,
Agatha Christie, H G Wells, Kipling, Georges
Simenon, and Edgar Wallace, if my poor
memory serves me well…'

'And, what are you grappling with now, another Wiley conundrum?'

'Not a word to a soul, I'm looking again at the Mata Hari affair…'

The band played some melodies from Cats, with long meows from the ladies.

Sara stopped in her tracks as she spotted Trueman flopped over in his chair. She sidled over.

'You OK, war hero?'

'Hmm. Ah it's my tablets, dropped one somewhere.'

'This blue one?'

'Yeah;

'Bit early in the evening for what did you say Viagra?'

'For sure, but it's just cramp-stop. Terrible at times when you're so tied up in a chair.'

'You must get into that para-Olympic stuff.'

'I do, I do: you are addressing the European champion at tiddlywinks on ice!'

'Indeed! Mind, happily the competition is not exactly stiff. That dance card filled up yet? I could do with a whirl round now they are tuning up for the salsa.'

'You're on Mr Trueman! You old dog. Shall I lead?'

'And not so much of the old, youngster, I'm not done yet.'

Sara twirled the chair round on its back wheels and shouted, 'Olez!'

'Robotics, you said, you're into.'

'Well AI in general and then we get on to the practicals making up new toys.'

She did a double turn and roll back.

'Like a real-time board game: but what's your next book, robo-man,' she teased. Can't wait. The suspense is killing me….'

'New peninsular wars. Set in Saigon… well so far, but we might be moving on rather swiftly to Agalega, where there's a secret pact with India's nuclear surveillance bureau … But my dear Sara, it's all terribly hush hush. Not a word to anyone. Can't have my plots kidnapped before they reach the Kindle screens.'

'I am thirteen tomorrow, Mr Trueman. I must be home by midnight.'

He caught her hand, easing her to him, whispering in her ear, 'Watch out for your father; and his new cricketing friends at the Mosque: they're listed.' She sensed his pulsing anxiety and the faint aroma of Eau de Cologne, and the momentary outline of his colostomy bag against her bosom, until he released her, chuckling as she tried another hands-free twirl on his strangely light-weight mobile chair. Titanium for sure, she mused, latest model for paralympic fencers.

She liked him a lot. Pity he's... Hm, but fun for a wrinkly, she brooded.

21. Lord's

It had rained on the Wednesday evening,
bringing out the soft perfumes from the old
English roses in the front gardens of the
formidable detached houses, as David made his
way, with his packed lunch in a knapsack,
passed Fenner's, where he had played for the
navy against the University, years before. He
had a lilt in his step as he mused on the other
times he had been to Lord's with his father,
seeing Botham in his prime and the elegance of
Gower. Yet he wondered if this trip would be so
full of joy, for there was something about
Abdulla's toast and the unexpected rôle that
had been thrust upon him as group leader.
Then, there was Imran, from the Punjab having
tickets for the match against his great cricketing
rivals India, of all things. 'Aren't they still
mortal enemies with memories that never die
from the great 1947 Partition in which so many
millions were slaughtered in religious
fanaticism, families vowing revenge to the nth

161

generation,' David pondered, as he strode on to
the rendezvous, buying a Times on the way to
read the Michael Atherton's cricket column. He
was in good time. It was yet 8.20 a.m. He had
done morning prayers at home with Sara and
Maryam who had planned a shopping trip to
town and would take the car. He felts uneasy,
without really knowing why, and kept
muttering, 'Trust no-one. Not even your
mother.'

That had been the training rule for
spooks. As he neared the Mosque, David
ruminated, feeling a strange quiver up his spine,
'Was it that thrill that he always felt when going
out to bat in the navy? Or was it the fear
brought on by those training interrogations and
that long deep bath filled with muck and all
those terrifying confrontations with foreign
spooks doomed to an early demise in his
hands.'
'Trust no-one not even yourself,'

He arrived early. He cast around and
caught in the corner of his eye a jogger, bending
down tying a shoe lace; and on the other side of

the street a woman, he had never seen before, selling posies of flowers. 'Am I being spooked?

Then one by one the others arrive on-time, exchanging warm Muslim greetings and traditional embraces. Igbal wearing a Turkish football jersey, for Galatessaray, of rich cherry red and orange yellow, Ismail looked rather smart in a college scarf and sweat shirt emblazoned with *I'm mad for Madingly*, Abdulla cheekily had an Egyptian Fez on his head. 'Assalaamualaikum!, guys, I've my lunch in this!' Hi!' Pointing to his head, he lifted the fez to reveal a sandwich box.

Then Imran drove up with the mini-van waving them to climb aboard. He had a GPS route already entered on his mobile fixed to the dashboard and beamed. David spotted the jogger, using his mobile and the woman flower seller had disappeared. 'Now, brothers this is the very day!'

On the uneventful journey south and through to St. John's Wood. Imran chatted twenty to the dozen as the others grabbed a little shut-eye and David wrestled with the

Times crossword. Imran even had a parking place in the basement of a nearby Pakistani restaurant where he knew the owner, a cousin, who greeted him warmly, hugged him firmly, whispered in his ear and had tears in his eyes as they disengaged.

'I'll be OK, inshallah, Sedek, my blessings on your family.'

As they passed through the turnstiles and strolled along the Nursery ground there were some Indian batsmen in the practice nets, David bought a scorecard to follow the day's play and to familiarise himself with the players on both teams. He was surprised when the others do not follow suit.

'We're a bit early so let's go to bookshop and store where we might find something to read or take back as gifts. I have a mate working there, might be some freebies,' Imran suggested, as they wandered further round the ground.

Passing the pavilion entrance there were two festive gentlemen sporting full MCC rig, with striped MCC ties, boaters and blazers, all in MCC colours. David spotted former England

164

stars, David Gower and Ian Botham, who were now part of the SKY sports commentary team. David and Imran moved over to them. David asked for their autographs on his scorecard and they obligingly agreed. They turned to Imran, asking him where he was from and which team he was supporting.

'Pakistan, so neither really, but I am looking forward to a great clash! See you on the box tonight for the highlights.'

'Have a fun day, good to see you all here,' chimed Gower, as with Botham, they bustled on to the commentary positions.

Getting to the bookshop Imran spotted his friend Sedek helping to unload boxes of books for sale. He chatted with him and other Pakistani workers. As Imran re-joined the group, Iqbal asked,

'Get anything to read at lunch-time Im?

'Imran waggled his head and smiled. How about this brand-new special offer back-pack, with super goodies for the great day! Gift from my friend.'

A large West Indian woman steward showed them to their seats in the Compton stand, and they settled themselves chatting as the umpires walked out from the pavilion, shortly followed by the England players who briskly took the field. The Indian captain had won the toss and decided to bat.

22. Arrest

As they chatted in their seats, David noticed the woman steward using her mobile, and nodding in their direction. Within seconds the Jumah Group were surrounded, taken to a side room, handcuffed and searched. In Imran's backpack they found a bomb, timer and primed suicide vest. Escape was fruitless as they saw more armed police crashing through the door shouting with automatic weapons drawn and full assault gear.

David was taken separately to an unmarked car, which had pulled up behind the Compton stand. They pushed him into the car, a bearded youth in jeans and a leather jacket reeking of tobacco put his hand on David's head to avoid any subsequent claim for assault. David glanced at his service issue watch that had a combined location chip, mobile phone and mpg voice recorder. He switched it on to send a quick SOS to Maryam and Sara to come and check with the police and get his lawyer there fast. He tapped a message to Sara, Checkout, 'Let Brooks try, with spin, MO.' A code? He left his phone on for sound recording the incident.

David was taken to the St John's Wood police station where he was formally arrested, read his rights and told they would be asking him questions about his links to terrorism offences and the plot to place explosives at the England India Test match. They do not say where his friends were in the Jumah group. Deep infiltration, but which one was on-side and why was he being locked up?

Reaching the station, David was bundled to an interview room where his intense interrogation continued over the next five days and nights. He asked for his London based lawyer, Peter Grant, who was there within the hour. A quietly spoken detective then read out a provisional charge of conspiracy to commit crime, namely to make and place explosives at Lord's cricket ground, Marylebone, London on Friday 23 June, with the intent to maim people and destroy private property etc., etc.

David went numb and could hardly hear the words in disbelief. Was MI6 setting him up? A detective inspector Davies then came in, introduced himself and read out a caution before asking David some questions. David signalled to Peter Grant, his lawyer and asked to go to the toilet, where under escort, he vomited and collapsed by the basin, sweating profusely. He felt for the issue strychnine pill he always carried for such extreme emergencies under the left lapel of his jacket, but they must have taken that when they stripped searched him. He wept and vomited again.

Why were they doing this to him. He searched in his mind for any textbook ruse that MI6 had laid out in their manual to be adopted to deflect enemy suspicion. Was it the old Nazi trick of shooting one of your friends, just to show your devotion to duty, and so disprove you had been turned and were a double agent?

He mumbled to himself the old adage, 'Trust no-one: neither your mother nor friends.' He knew that the MI6 rule was complete denial about any captured agent, cutting off any links to the centre when caught in politically embarrassing compromise. He wanted Sara and Maryam now. But was dragged off to another interrogation room with a bath filled with water. He fainted with the memory of the many captives he had pushed to the extreme point of no return, using baths such as this: Japanese, Koreans, the occasional Russian diplomat, and then grimaced at the thought of the US naval commander they had taken in with the oldest of all tricks, the honey trap, by that dark skinned Philippine dancer. That yank had actually drowned himself, purposely breathing in the water rather than struggling to survive the brutality.

Now, David was wandering his thoughts turned to the Inquisition that had shown Galileo the instruments of torture and he had declined for twenty years to publish his mind-blowing astronomy observations on the movement of the moon, sun and the planets. David asked himself what could be the sacrifice to save his own skin, Maryam, Sara, his body, his mind.

He held out for five days of intense interrogation, his lawyer threatening to lodge a case in the European court of Human Rights. He was dished up horrendously loud high pitched deafening sounds more like screeches; irregular meals and continually waking if he fell asleep; standing in stress positions with his arms held outstretched for fear of being beaten,

At the end of this time, he was formally charged and surprisingly released on bail of £50,000, which he was told a friend had paid for him. They did not say who. David suspected double dealing. Desmond must have had doubts over the security risks if David had been turned by ISIS. His trial was coming up in four weeks, in camera, no press no jury, and no public, at the request of the Home Office.

23. Trial

When the case opened David pleaded not guilty to the charges of terrorism against him, claiming he was an accidental witness to the plot to plant bombs at Lord's and would have contacted the police as soon as he discovered anything suspicious. The Court dismissed his claims finding strong evidence against him with photos of him in the company of known terrorists and a tape recording of him agreeing to join them. David realised that the group had already been infiltrated by MI6 and cursed Desmond for not having warned him. There was no point in him claiming he was also a member of MI6 as that would be officially denied. The explosives they had found, in what was described as his hide, were identical to those in Imran's back-pack. They were a design David had been trained to make and use on his course with SOE in Scotland and had his finger prints all over them. Curious all that. There was

172

also evidence presented of his time in Syria and he admitted he had converted and married a Syrian ISIS member, Maryam.

David fell into a daydream as the court proceedings rumbled on. Deep down he knew he was an anarchist manqué: he had increasingly become aware that the life in Intelligence was but a cover for his natural bent. He passed his right hand over his tight light brown hair and whimpered to himself as he looked back into his past as a life chasing an illusion not a dream. His childhood had been so protected and pre-planned as the eldest son of an architect, Marcus, whose firm specialised in new towns. Marcus had put David's name down for Marlborough college the day he was born and told him that Trinity College Cambridge would follow.

That was the era when architects were admired, they were as boon to society, enriched the built environment with pleasant workable structures pleasing the eye and well suited to their place in the scheme of things. His father was comfortably off, content with his achievements,

173

with an OBE for his work on the rehabilitation of mining towns and anxious to pass on to the next generation the style and comforts he enjoyed. He was a free-church man and a traditional liberal with a patrician calm about him that encouraged veneration and respect. He had endowed David with a little portfolio of shares that he could play with on his eight birthday and kept a desk for him warm in his City architectural offices that he expected David to occupy in the fullness of time. Yet David had spoiled all those plans by opting for Sussex and Dartmouth and never looked back, despite his father's discomfort and his mother's tears when he left in his naval uniform.

As the Court resumed its session after lunch, David's thoughts turned to his mother, Sylvia, who had cherished him dearly. She was a graduate in English from Oxford. After her early marriage to his father Marcus, she had re-tracked her life into guiding the education of her two children, David and his younger sister Emma. She had displaced her gift of spell binding energy, when they were both at

174

boarding schools, into an unnerving clutch of committees, saving young women from sin, protecting the flora and fauna of rural Britain, supervising a florid team in an adult literacy programme for the working-class mothers of the neighbourhood. They had scant knowledge of words beyond the local market place and the free chapels, but. her pupils wanted to read the Daily Mirror, their utility bills, their stars, and their children's school reports.

Sylvia sang contralto in a choral group that did the Messiah at Christmas, including the Easter music, Gilbert and Sullivan in the Spring and a musical in the summer, raising money for cancer charities. This she immensely enjoyed, admixed with a vivid exchange of the local gossip, of broken engagements, divorces, abortions, plastic surgery and urological complications amongst the ageing tenors and bases. She once had her bottom caressed by the lead baritone in Sound of Music when she wasn't looking. She had thought, maybe, he was checking to see if she was wearing underclothes: but she attracted no further approaches even when she was enticingly uncovered underneath, how did they say in France, sans culottes.

Since having a family, she had found few of the outlets for her suppressed intellectual energy or for stirring the world as she had in the Pankhurst Society. She had reformed this at Oxford, as a voice for human rights with its radical wing against bonded labour and the exploitation of college migrant domestic and kitchen staff. She had been warned off by her tutor. You could be sacrificing a first, she advised. She withdrew from the forays of political action but still only managed to get a second and distrusted advice from dons ever since.

David had loved her dearly and it was one of the ironies of life that she was taken with cancer of the bowel so young and tended by people from one of her dedicated charities for support to the terminally ill in her last days, being laid to rest by the graves of her own parents in Frome.

David had been determined to fulfil the promise to his mother as she had drifted away.

Then David collapsed to the floor as he realised he was dropping off. He pinched his thigh, took deep breaths and rehearsed his old coding key, 'The life that I have...' As he came round from his day dreams, David looked about and saw the Judge motioning for him to stand, as he read out his brief summing up. Guilty as charged, sentence deferred for reports. 'All rise!' And the judge, who looked for all-the-world like a Shakespearian actor whose name David could not remember, departed.

Eventually the verdict was delivered: five years to be served in Whitemoor Prison, in March, Cambridgeshire. A category A high security prison with a majority of dangerous Muslim inmates and terrorists. David was a disgraced and betrayed defector.

24. **Whitemoor Prison**

They took him in a heavily barred and guarded police wagon to Whitemoor, stopping off at Cambridge Police station for a lunch of meat slops and old bread, which he could hardly stomach. The toilets were a disgrace with pools of urine over the floor and the pedestal with no seat, a flush that did not work, no soap and a trickle of water from the tap above, a cracked and dirt encrusted basin that had not been cleaned for months. This was just a taste of the sordid life that would be his, he guessed, in notorious Whitemoor, top place for the incarceration of the most notorious criminals, none there for less than 5 years.

Finally, they arrived at Whitemoor, set in a wilderness, miles from any other habitation and with heavy military style armed security and vicious looking Alsatian dogs. He was strip searched, with exploration of every orifice for concealed weapons drugs or valuables. His smart watch was confiscated as well as his wedding ring and all his personal possessions. He was forced to use the evil smelling toilet which had no door for privacy and was overlooked by surveillance cameras. He showered under close supervision. He was roughly shaved of his proud beard and moustache. His light brown hair was removed with a razor leaving him totally bald, save for the cuts the pitiless barber had left which bled and had to be staunched with tough pads dipped in sharp antiseptic and then plasters like a patchwork quilt across his bare pate. He changed into heavy boots and rough sewn heavy linen prisoner's garb in blue and white stripes.

David was pushed into a single room where he was told he would be in solitary confinement as a dangerous terrorist, with one hour per day supervised exercise in the prison yard. For good behaviour he might be allowed, after one year, to join one of the work gangs breaking rocks on the moor.

He asked for reading and writing materials but was refused. He had no means of telling the time. There was a small thick glass window at the top of the wall of his cell but with high illumination lights outside, and it now being winter, it was difficult even to detect whether it was night or day. Foul smelling food came intermittently through the grill in the heavy steel door. There was another evil smelling toilet with no seat in the cell; another cracked wash basin with a small basic bar of soap, and a much used and a dirty looking ragged towel. No mirror, no electrical sockets, and just an iron bed with slatted iron springs, a filthy looking mattress, probably infested with bed bugs, evidence of rat mess in one corner and the pervasive odour of urine.

He paced the cell from side to side: ten feet, by eight feet with a ceiling of probably fourteen feet. Built of solid stone blocks hewn from the craggy moor two hundred years before, there were some vestiges of paintwork of a dull grey tinge with a dark green border at floor level – or was that mould? He wanted to write, to read to talk to someone. Nothing. It would be nothing, every day for a year or more. He was denied visitors. He was trapped and consumed with guilt and suicidal sweaty spasms that left him exhausted and weeping.

David thought back to his training to resist all pressure and even torture. Yet, this nothingness, was worse and he had not been prepared for that. Perpetual silence. Not a bird, nor the wind, nor traffic. Shouts or even screams in pain and desolation he could have welcomed. Just nothing. Nothing. Then more of the same nothing stretching out into the distant future. And yet there was a spider silently weaving its web. He watched it with relief that he at least had one companion. And that spider was busy plotting his own survival by making a trap for any careless fly that might come past. David saw that there was just one small such creature already trapped in the web. Was that his own fate, to be expended, disgraced in the dark system of punishment for defectors and traitors, doomed like the fly to a solitary end.

He lay in his bed and wept, repelled by his life that had brought him to this lowest of the low ends. He blamed himself for being led into this world of covert shadows where nothing was real and fear was his continuing reality. Even in his sleep he was not free from such fear and personal guilt which he dreaded would burst his head, like an assassin's shot with an explosive shell, spattering his brain in one splurge of blood and vessels like JFK in that motorcade in Dealey Plaza, downtown, Dallas Texas. He trembled and shook with fear, rage and remorse that he had seemingly been trapped and betrayed his country, his family, his new wife and his lovely daughter. He was shivering and wanted to vomit as others had done over the grey walls of the cell.

He could feel himself sliding into the depths of self-pity, self-hate and abject cowardice. Then he recalled the H G Wells story he had read to Sara, the History of Mr Polly, which revered hope, even for the prisoner who with systematic fasting could change the dull walls of his prison cell to at least the more hygienic circumstance of the sick bay.

A day and a night he thought had passed. David's mind wondered across his favourite memories, as a child, picking strawberries with his mother; his first time really swimming; the girl who said she loved him when he was just seventeen; cracking the Talban military code. Then he set himself the exercise to eliminate those cherished moments from his mind so as to prepare himself for his fate. He had been fighting other people's wars for so long, yet he was left with the unremitting guilt for adding his quota to the world's untimely dead: his mind became lost in the shadows of his past. He used to think he could escape his fears: now he knew it was remorse that stole assiduously into his most unguarded moments.

Then came scraping and tap, tapping on the walls. Faint, but clear enough. Was it Morse? Not English; nor French. Yes, it could be Arabic. Scraping, what? Surely not? A Surah! Al fatiha. The opening of the Koran and indeed of every

183

time of prayer. He wept again as he realised how neglectful he had been of his prayers. Self-indulgent, miserable offender. He prayed too that he might at least receive God's mercy, despite the world seeing him as a notorious defector and traitor, maligned in the eyes of all, with total ignominy his fate.

The grill opened, the keys turned, the door swung open. An overweight, dark haired smelly guard stamped in, pushing him to one side, checked his bed and slammed the door closed again without a word or gesture, no eye contact. Nothing more, after he had heard the rasp of the key being turned and the grill being slammed down. He was banged up for the night, and then it would be night after night, with no relief: Just this perpetual nothingness.

25. Hoax

His cell door clanged open as David was doing his daily exercise regimen after his evening prayers, quietly singing to himself, the old marching song, 'It's a long way to Tipperary, it's a long way to go... in his sorrowful resonant baritone voice...to the sweetest girl I know...'

Desmond entered breezily. 'Hi! Sailor! We have some work for you!'

'Go away, Archer! It's all finished: I'm thinking of ending it all! What the hell are you doing here, Des, you bloody crook?'

'Come on David, it was all a set up. The fake group, the arrest, the interrogation the court, your transfer here in Manchester Grenada

185

film studios. All scenes you've been through have been part of our cover story for you, as a disgraced defector. Surely you rumbled dear Alec Malt as the Judge! It was just a bit of MI6 theatre to get you operational again. Look he pressed a button and the grey walls of the prison slid open to reveal a panorama of people, trucks and studios in the midst of feverish activity making TV shows. The height of the sun showed it was around mid-day, not night time, with a jostling crowd of technical staff and actors moving in and out of the adjacent studios milling around for they daily work. Desmond handed David the smart watch that had been confiscated on his arrival at Whitemoor.

David landed a fierce punch to Desmond's midriff and a hand-chop to his neck. It was the great irony of this shadowy life: you were never betrayed by an enemy. His good friend Des, folded over, collapsing to the floor, laughing.

After a night at the art deco Gotham Hotel in King's Street Manchester, a change of clothes and a splendid meal, the next morning they flew together to a military airfield near Dartmouth, then by fast car to the naval College. There in a seminar room David had his briefing for operation Caliph rendition, to locate and despatch the ISIS leaders to the Chagos islands for interrogation and their final rites before joining Osama Ben Laden as one of the great has-beens of history. This would be triggered once the remnants of ISIS who escaped from the shattered Mosul, and scurried to whatever safe holes they could find, were rounded up by the Allies and the principal ISIS palace guards dispersed or turned.

Meanwhile David could return to Sheer where Maryam and Sara were celebrating the EID ul Ada festival, aka the feast of Abraham. David had been theatrically incarcerated for just six weeks, a price he was determined to have repaid when the time was ripe. He reluctantly signed up for the mission, committing himself to total secrecy: what else could he do? Then he was whisked away in a limousine back to rural Sussex and the life he would cherish all the more, if only too briefly.

The Defector's Daughter

26. Apostate

Sara turned to her diary; those very first pages again: the panic dream with the helical stairway, where all was up-side-down and she could not find her way to the Senate House and that strange gardener with the oddest boots. She started writing:

Extract from Sara's diary
August 13 20//
Lol! Lol! Just chill being back with Dad,
Oops!

She lurched to one side as David swerved his classic Jensen Interceptor S to avoid a crow hopping up from some tasty morsel crushed on the road, maybe a hedgehog. Her seat belt tight on her slight body brought her back to the level again as the car retained its position in the overtaking lane. But she had smudged her fresh page in the diary and left a black ink mark on her royal blue skirt.

David was driving fast along the A3. He just loved the surge of power from the 7.2 litre engine and the splendid vision from the sloping wrap-round rear window. What a great gift this had been in the legacy from his father's brother who had run the sports car showroom in West Bromwich which he had visited many times to have free test runs in some of the extraordinary galaxy of super-powered racers. The Interceptor was not exactly promised to him on his last visit when his uncle said he himself was getting too old for the fast track and David was a tad too young. But then when the Will was read....

As he sailed round the next bend, using his heel and toe for the manoeuvre balancing the revs and wheel rotation, he caught a glance of Sara's latest outfit as she sat slumped in the passenger seat, inclined back to allow her to snooze. Micro skirt, showing the full length of her slender legs. Just a slip of a girl. But razor sharp. A rather scruffy, un-ironed off-white top with a low hanging neckline that indicated no bra: what was the world coming too; of course, no white gloves and no hat, that had been de rigueur in his youth; green tinted hair or was it a green wig; two studs in her purple shaded eyebrows; emerald green flat pumps with laces, what did she call them, Converse Top Stars, or was it All Stars? And then the Che Ghavera T-shirt with Tania Bunke knap-sack, from the Sofia Youshia stable, resting on her lap. Quite a chick!

'Take the round-about without braking', she looked up from her mobile and challenged him. 'Wow! Let's have a ton up on the straight.'

She felt the surge of power as he opened the full throttle of his racing engine to 80, 90, 95 and 100, slowing a little to shimmy through the next junction in top gear. David's time on the circuits of Brand Hatch with the Navy team, testing secret service vehicles, had not been wasted. Now they were in the last stretch before they entered the Cambridge urban area. Come on Dad, another screamer!'

But David was changing down through the gears, as he saw in his mirror through the Interceptor's wide-view rear window an ambulance with siren raging moved swiftly past, to join a haggle of an emergency posse of fire, police, ambulance and army armoured cars attending a blazing foray of tangled hot metal and hollering crews one hundred yards ahead. He stopped the engine, opened the door, striding towards the mêlée at the scene. He flashed his service card to the senior police officer.

'What do we have here then?'

'Road side bomb, Sir'

'Target?'

'We're...'

Then from behind the shrubberies that skirted the free-way, leapt a huge black masked figure, with a motor-bike helmet and shaded visor wielding a flashing sabre.

'For you, apostate, for you!'

David primed from his training days in armed combat, dives and rolls under the armoured car, pulling his favourite Sig Sauer P230 from his discreet shoulder holster, hitting the armed attacker with three targeted shots: to the knees, stomach and chest. The police inspector calls for back-up over his mobile phone, moving as he does so onto the blood-soaked attacker to disarm him, when the whole scene explodes with body parts scattering in the smoke of a detonated suicide bomb. Fluorescent hot metal arches over the scene, the acrid smell of cordite in the air, its toxic gas choking David's lungs, as he lies in shock beneath the armoured vehicle that he fears might ignite at any moment, but unable to shift his body into any movement as the sulphurous fumes envelop all around. Shouting and more gunfire, glass flying, the clunk of boots hitting the tarmac as more emergency and military personnel take action in a spontaneous terrifying counter attack.

Sore, safe, but sickened by the battlefield violence, Sara, shaking uncontrollably, slips from her seat in the car, peering through the dense smog, searching for what might be left of her father in the chaos that appalled her.

'Hey, there Dad, you OK, … can't see you. Where are you? Answer me!'

David's ears are scarcely picking up any sounds, just a muffled buzzing. He fears his eardrums had burst with the impact of the bomb and the shooting. His face is bleeding, and one eye closed, when he had hit gravel on the road where the armoured car was parked. He smells diesel leaking from somewhere and a slick edging its way towards him with the camber of the road. A cat's eye marker on the road shattered into fragments, catches his left hand, he sees shadowy figures approaching with raised weapons pointing at him. He recognises the short stock of the C8 carbine used by SAS and other mobile special units. And then the outline emerging from the smoke cloud of an unmistakable Blue Dolphin anti-terror helicopter, of the sub-group of the celebrated 22nd SAS rapid action regiment.

'Welcome guys but what are you doing here? David growls as he casts his still hot and smoking P230 to the ground, thinking, 'Must have intercepted a planned ambush and come from other manoeuvres close at hand. Their base is way over at Credenhill, in Hertfordshire.

The major leading the squad comes over, checks David is OK and calls on his Hi-Tech

SAS style walkie-talkie for the field ambulance team to attend.

'What happened?'

'Just stopped on traffic and then, all hell broke loose. Hit the guy with three shots from my P230 and then woooof! Up he went in smoke taking the police inspector with him.'

'We had a tip off. In the area on a training practice about to return to Credenhill, when this all hit.'

He turns towards Sara, as she heard the talking and wanted to ask if anyone had seen her dad.

'Nothing to see here Miss. Better go back to your car.'

'But that's my dad there. Dad you're bleeding. You OK?

She rushes to him, but is stopped by the major.

'Sorry Miss. He needs expert help.' Please stand back.

The team medic reaches David first and does a quick triage.

'Walking wounded here, but get a stretcher he's in deep shock.'

The field ambulance team firmly raise David onto the stretcher and into a fresh ambulance that has just arrived at the incident.

'Can a driver take you to follow our car into Cambridge Miss. The Addingdale Hospital, know it?

Sara kisses her father, thanks the field team and walks back to the car still parked well away from all the debris. The police wave her driver through who tucks in behind the ambulance as it moves off with David safely on board. Sara does some idle hacking, her newest hobby, to see who's doing whom.

****

Transcript Sara intercepted from audio record of meeting at HQ Counter terror, London
HQ Anti-terror: Partisan
5/26

M.O: Plan C now, yeah? Ambush botched. Where do we get these people from? Number 4 asset just got wasted. Up in smoke. SAS buggers turned up. Who the fuck called them in? We'll have to extract number 5, with the SAS there in force.

There'll be a bloody Inquiry of course. But we can pull rank on that. Now go to it Archer. Adapt C. Off to that hospital emergency ward. Your assets still in place?

D.A. Yes, Ma'am.

M.O. (Muffled) Then, arsehole, how many times do we have to do this? And Archer, I want a clean job. No collateral damage. No loose ends. Got it. Go!

D.A. (Very faint) …Ma'am.

Note: added to file by M.O. bring-forward 2 weeks (initialled M.O with red sticker)

M.O I wonder if I have had enough of this: should ask for a transfer

T.R It's been a long day Ma'am.

M.O. You know Timothy, I've been covering my back for five years now and increasingly wonder how I can survive any more of those in-depth screenings they have had since the Cambridge five. Then there are my nightmares about giving away something muttering to myself in the staff room. Unearthing the past. Often think back to those days in the Ukraine.

The dancing and Spring flowers after tough winters.

T.R. Sh's Ma'am, CCTV and sound devices everywhere, and turned on, these days, Ma'am, M.O. On now? Bloody hell what crap is that? (Mobile on with music: muffled whispers). (Bugger me it's... Archer... trust... (Very faint, music louder)...Zac.. to go after Shit (*Possibly Brand (or Band*). (Then music stops) Christ! What a tangled web...! (Sound off).

Sara muses. Time to see Emma. Looks like Dad's into a post truth omnishambles

27.   Emma

Extract from Sara's diary

May 30 20?? waiting, waiting in this god forsaken hole in some drab corridor outside Dad's private room for VIPs in the professorial trauma unit. I fumble in my Che Guevara sleeve for a tissue to clean off my running mascara, as I write this entry. Could be one of those times. Trust no-one, but Emma F2F. Not to worry Dad now with this intercept, IMHO!

Sara starts flipping through the leaves of the past two tumultuous years. Then flicks through her mobile to edit out old messages and hits on that enigmatic one from her father. Possibly a code. She thinks she will discuss it with Emma or Geoffrey at Russell, when she has a moment. Maybe he can spot a key or run it through his system. Maybe he even has an idea about MO.

She goes back to her journal. Reading from her past entries

Extracts from Sara's diary

4 January 20?? Copenhagen

The purpose of this personal journal, I have decided is to record my feelings about growing up after the awesome unplugging of my ears. Can now hear a pin drop, birds' song, toilet flushing, bicycles near, direction light in car clicking and soft voices of love and temptation. Worried sick about Dad and think I am on to some dirty tricks. He never says a word about his work. Hush, Hush, but the hints from Emma over the past months when we have got getting close, Dad away, after weird stuff in Budapest. Hope he's OK. That Holmes' coded SMS. Could be anywhere trapped. Desmond never helpful at best, vague. Not sure I entirely trust him keeps looking at me in a strange way. OMG just hope Dad's safe, rather took him for granted. Never again. Wan 2 get his hugs and quiet support.

3/ January 20??

*With Emma all day. Sh's OTT mostly. Super
fun today Royal Porcelain works and then
got me roller blades to move around with
her. Sh's an ace on hers and bringing me
along. Scream, scream screaming along the
tracks, stuffing the blades on knapsack for
coffee and marinated fish with capers and
lager beer.*

Sara flipped through some more recent
entries in her journal as she slipped from dozing
into wakefulness and back again, half dreaming,
half aware of the scene about her in the corridor
of her life, stretching forward and back with
Emma and her teddy bear as comforters when
David was away. Her dry tearfulness turned
about in her wandering mind at the continual
wrenching of her days from despair to
continued hope for a better way ahead, barely
expressed in words and more like silent
extemporary prayers.

Extract from Sara's diary
June 2 20??

The Hay book festival with Emma. Never too much butter. Had a lift from Emma back home. She chatted about being a tutor at Cambridge, lectures, punting, parties, May Ball...She wants me to go up soon and wld mentor me exploring the future. GR8. Wants me to stay a week or more with her - get me through A levels, starting in two weeks! And then the entrance exam- Never too young she said. Her silk blouse I remember was sicking to her nipples. No bra. I'm just into my first with lace and some padding, but why, she asked. Feel free as air. She smokes pot and has given up fags. Showed me the first edition of Seven Pillars of wisdom she had picked up at Hay. Two grand. Told her you can get a paperback one for nothing these days. Says Lawrence was into SDM, liked being beaten up by the boys in the Air force unit he joined after his time in the desert and the Arab revolt. Takes all sorts. Not my rave. Tho I do wonder sometimes about all that, sex stuff. Odd dreams some nights...

Sara dosed again. Then flipped through the pages of her journal to where Emma had taken her through Russell's efforts on symbolic language and his sudden expulsion from Trinity when he published pamphlets against the war with Germany siding with those who saw war as the great illusion. Even the brilliant Hardy had not been able to save him. She passed over her note on Hardy and his disciple Ramanujan, the Indian village maths genius who had startled the whole of the Trinity set and whose notebooks were still exciting post grads even now with their sheer originality.

Extract from Sara's diary
June 4 20??
Awesome stuff. Quite a 3sum, Russell, Hardy and Ramanujan, not to mention Littlewood for whom Emma seemed to have a special place in her list of math's greats to follow. Maybe cos he went into the army and the others were against all wars. Emma has been involved in some hush, hush army stuff, I think. Never says a word tho.

The scent of hospital disinfectant wafted across the pages of her diary as she mused about the extraordinary transformation in her life and mind, egged on by Emma's racy style, spilling out with elaboration after elaboration on ideas Sara had half encountered in her former secluded life with her fascination for numbers. The starlings were leaving for the town centre, squalling as they left in mass flight.

David opened the one eye he could see through, the other closed with a reddening bruise and gash from his hasty encounter with the gravel under the armoured truck. He saw Sara looking through the window of the door, smiling sweetly at him. He beckoned her in. She checked no nurses about and eased through the half-opened door to the private room. She thought fine for peace, but a risk of neglect or even attack from these terrorists who seemed to be after her father. Why? What had he done to them? She did not know. He did not tell: she would never ask. Their family secret. Dad's job was just off limits.

He had dropped off again and was thrashing about with his arms as if fighting off an invisible assailant. He seemed to be silently shouting, sweating profusely. The mask was muffling his words if there were any. He knocked the bedside table and an empty flowerpot crashed to the ground, scattering broken porcelain across the tiled floor. A nurse rushed in. Checked David was fine and demanded, 'And who are you? No visitors until after the consultant's round. I'm afraid you will have to go outside. And any way he needs a bed bath and toileting, so...'

Sara blew David a kiss, pouted at the nurse, flouncing out in her best imitation of an unbridled teenager. She sat on one of the plastic chairs in the corridor and started to write up her journal for that turbulent day. But started crying and shaking so she could hardly hold the pen.

'Hello! Are you waiting for admission?' It was a tall doctor in a long white coat, stethoscope hanging loosely around his neck. He bent down and looked into her eyes, lifting her right hand and feeling her rapid pulse and her clammy hands. 'Hm! Have you had an accident or a fall?'

'Well not really. It's my dad in there. Been attacked. Gun shots and explosion. They killed the policeman blowing themselves up. Awesome! Horrible.'

She burst into uncontrollable tears and tremors engulfing her whole slight frame.

'What's your name?'

'Sara Brand. That's my father in there, Commander Brand. He's been badly hit, I think. I just escaped...'

'I'm Dr. Hawkins, and I am just going to exam your dad, but I think you may be in shock and I will ask the nurse to have a look at you next. Stay as still as you can, breathe deeply and I'll get someone to bring you a blanket to keep you warm in this rather draughty corridor.'

The nurse opened the door for him.

'While I am examining Commander Brand can you get a blanket for Sara outside, I think she is in shock too and may need to be put under observation. See if there's a trolley around and get her to lie down with her feet raised a little.

Now Commander Brand, how are you doing? Nasty business.'

Sara's troubled mind leapt back to that afternoon, in the late summer, when Emma had taken her fruit picking in an orchard garden belonging to Madingly Hall. But she had difficulty focusing as she remembered standing amidst the sumptuous Cambridgeshire countryside; the college nestled along a narrow lane within a village where the arc of the sky seemed so immense and the honey bees were in the shrubberies. The ornate topiary freshly trimmed. In the meadow beyond the ha ha, the Friesian cows sought the shade of the massive Chestnuts and cedars of Lebanon: a scenic paradise. Sara shivered as the nurse put a light blanket around her shoulders and loosened the belt around her waist.

'Just try to keep calm and breathe more deeply,' the nurse advised as she took her pulse and looked into Sara's staring eyes.'

'Madingly… yes Madingly.' Sara's mind wandered 'What was it, now?' She tried to gaze across that memory of that day with Emma.

207

When something had just happened. 'What was it?' She had been puzzled by that for weeks.

Madingly was fashioned centuries before by Capability Brown, the father of landscape gardening; his mission to bring cultivated nature into the aspect from the stone mullioned windows of the Elizabethan hunting lodge, now serving its time as a postgraduate college of education. Unforgettable: that English summer idyll with Emma, lazing in the meadow, their bodies touching. Then Bang! On the A3 blown apart by the bombers. But Sara searched around her mind, disjointed as it was as she shivered again and the nurse carried her onto a trolley, covering her loosely with a blue blanket. Not quite the colour to go with her green hair style! She pulled the blanket over her head and curled up sucking her right thumb.

'Where had that calm gone to?' she just needed it now: to find that calm again as the tremors passed through her body once more and she wept in pity for herself, her father and the world that could do all this horror. She felt faint and deathly cold as the nurse took her hand and comforted her again passing her soft strong hand over Sara's head and face and talking quietly to her.

'OK now? You just fainted a little. I'll stay with you while doctor decides whether you need to be admitted.' 'But where had Emma gone?' Sara slipped in and out of consciousness, comforted by the nurse's quiet words.

28. Madingly Hall

During the summer Sara, Maryam and Emma cared for David, on a loose kind of shift system. Maryam was the sister in charge seeing to all David's needs as he slowly recovered, taking short walks in the garden at Cambridge and preparing his favourite summer foods. He delighted in the smoked trout salads and trifle with fresh strawberries.

Maryam encouraged Sara and Emma to take a break away for the house. They would often go to Madingly Hall where Emma had rooms, or punting on the Cam, playing tennis, watching some cricket at Fenner's. They delighted on the fine days of outings in Emma's open-top mini-cooper. Some afternoons they took tea and scones at Emma's house, Hollyhocks. It was in the village close to the Madingly Hall. Or they would go to Russell College where Emma was a seasoned post graduate tutor in mathematics and cryptology

210

for largely an international intake of students on secondment from military service.

Emma's huge, Nigerian, athletic house-guest Gordon Mckenzie was always discreet and would go for a run when they arrived, bringing back groceries from the village shop, by the Hall. He was fun at supper asking Sara about her studies and telling her about village life in Nigeria where he grew up. He was clearly devoted to Emma and she to him and he would creep quietly around the house when Sara went up to sleep in the spare room; but she would hear joyous giggling from their room when Emma and he sang folk songs and made love into the small hours.

It was her happiest time as Sara was blossoming into a vivacious and special teenager, fearless in the erudite dinners Emma took her to with senior College staff, always holding her own in argument, quizzing the leading lights on their latest research; yet she was charming and informal with the many post-graduates who mingled at Hollyhocks for afternoon tea on Tuesdays and Thursdays. She wondered if she was likely to fall in love with this life with Emma: Gordon she just admired from afar, sometimes ogling at his massive muscles, rippling under his skin tight jeans and sweat shirts and yet his quiet soft manner.

Emma chatted with her about her domestic life, one day during a restful moment under the willows, at Madingly, with the scent of honeysuckle attracting the Red Admiral butterflies as it wafted in the air. They had been punting on the Cam, seeking some shade from the hot afternoon sun, when Emma explained to Sara about her personal life, woman to woman. Gordon was the son of a Scottish engineering father, Robert Mckenzie, who had been in Nigeria on some oil project and fell for a young Nigerian girl, Christabel, who was the caterer for the crew. They married but tragically she had died giving birth to Gordon when they had been together just two years; so, Gordon was reared by her grandmother, Ibukun, a local pharmacist, before Robert was recalled to his company in Glasgow, where Gordon went to school.

Emma explained that, before they met, Gordon actually had a young son in Glasgow, Bruce; the child is a few years older than Sara, and wanted to read engineering like his grandfather. Gordon did geology, maths and anthropology, a strange mix, as he was planning to return to his native country and link up with his grandmother's family, but he was waylaid by a young Scottish lass. They lived together for some years but eventually she went off to the South-Seas, on a research project in oceanography and they broke up leaving Bruce with Gordon who adored him.

'I met Gordon at a Peace conference in Paris five years ago. He's now into maths and cryptology too having done a post-grad course in London.'

'He's rather formidable, Emma, Wow!'

'Yep! Not just in codes. Can't deny the basic facts of life there!'

'A manly man! Oh aunt!'

They giggled, rocking the punt splashing in the water that sloshed over their feet as they enjoyed the moment.

'Sara you are too young for that!'

'No, I am just growing up and reading D H Lawrence! You must explain the rude bits to me sometime.' Emma gave her a knowing look, They burst into peels of girlish laughter that attracted enquiring glances from a couple of undergrads, struggling with their punt to avoid the overhanging willow branches.

'Actually Sara, he is a great comfort to me in times of stress. Big men can be very quiet and soothing. Perhaps you would like to meet Bruce, his boy, who is doing well at school and expected to get all A stars next year and go on to university.

Extract from Sara's diary

Dad's making strides and just love's being with Maryam who coos to him and holds his hand warmly in hers, smiling gently as he regains his strength and purpose. While, with Emma, we gorged on mulberries this wknd from a grotesque tree that looked as if at been there for ever. (Must check if that T shirt is dry: put it on the line after breakfast.) It's by the crumbling old kitchen garden wall, at Madingly, its branches cradling the loose stones and some trailing over the remnants of a summer house on one of those tracks so you could swivel it round to catch the sun. But now the rails are overgrown with ivy and it just serves to offer shelter to some dilapidated deck chairs. There is also a rambling grenadine in a sheltered spot by the wall facing south with awesome mauve and white flowers. Emma says the fruit are cool. And then she told me about the figs which will be ripe soon, espaliered across an ancient oak trellis. Emma says when they are ripe and you ease them open to reveal their pink and scarlet interior, soft and warm from the sun, they are a sensation to the throat and tongue sucking and licking into the bitter sweet yielding layers that exude their juices round your mouth. Must try some of that with Trixie when she's back from Greece with family. But I never got Emma on to the decrypt. She seems to change the subject when I try to talk about what Dad does and his chums and the dangers...

215

What's the time, even the date?

Some days later

OMG, we have been in a deluxe quality sojourn. But now Dad's quite recovered and been recalled to duty whatever that is. We are missing him already. The call came yesterday and he is off to the airport to rush over to Budapest. But I have a queer feeling all is not well and cried myself to sleep with teddy between my legs for some comfort. More anon...

Time passes...

29. Triple Jeopardy

David flew back to Budapest after a long leave, not sure if he was ready yet for more active service and wondering if he was following the plot that Desmond has devised for him: screening migrants from diverse war zones for ISIS terrorists. He loathed leaving Sara and Maryam with more tearful goodbyes at the door of Peartree Cottage.

'Back soon, inchallah.'

'Keep safe, this time and in touch every day, or we will worry our hearts out, darling!'

Sara squeezed his hand and rested her head on his arm. He kissed them both and hugged them to his chest, suppressing the tears that welled in his eyes, ruefully regretting his calling that had caused so much pain. He hoped he could gather up just enough courage to put his family before his country. He felt, he was about to be severely tested again. He knew the risks, but declined to confront his fears, trapped with that recurring uneasy conscience.

His love had grown for Sara, after her sudden liberation and remarkable metamorphosis. He relished the romance with Maryam who saved him from the brutal assassins of ISIS. Strange how those days had flown. Sara has been at Russell College, now, for two years, having completed her degree in record time. She was all but 14 and registered for a postgrad course leading to a doctorate, still chaperoned by Maryam when in Cambridge.

David, momentarily switched away from the warm soft kisses and hugging. He had to focus on his new mission. He had to try to link up again with the various agents he had been handling.

30. Bombed in Budapest

Then he was on the plane again and touching down in Budapest. He idly checked his jacket for any note that might have been slipped into his pocket by ISIS, as before, when he was kidnapped. And he dwelt on the curious behaviour of Zac and Desmond, He arrived at the book shop, key in hand, opened the lock and was enveloped in debris from an explosion, primed by the key as he turned it in the lock. David was wounded, but not gravely. He slipped away, to avoid the crowd that had assembled after the explosion, and heard the sound of the emergency services signalling their arrival. In the confusion of fallen masonry and passers-by stopping and crowding in, he managed to stumble away, making it back to his flat in his ripped and bloodstained clothes torn by the bomb. In the bathroom he checked his wounds, all superficial, but blood still oozing from a deep cut on his scalp. He bound on a makeshift head bandage from a bath towel to stem the flow. Always amazed at how scalp wounds, even quite trivial can bleed so freely. It's just in movies and novels, the heroes get beaten with iron bars and end up in hospital with a sticking plaster over their forehead. He puked into the basin and fell gradually to the ground. This is not the way to start a new assignment. Had he been fitted-up? Was that a warning or a failed attempt to do him in. Who? Which side? Was this another hoax by Desmond. Or were ISIS onto him for not doing their bidding. Not their double agent; but turned and now a triple agent, hunted by both sides.

David mused on what were the chances of surviving the crossfire. Not good, he thought as he fell into a post-traumatic coma.

It was some three days later that David found he was recovering from his wounds with Emma and Sara in his flat in Budapest looking after him. They had failed to reach him on his mobile, checked his security monitors in his flat and saw him not moving on the floor, head heavily bandaged. Emma arranged the next flight from Heathrow and they were there within four hours, gaining entry with a spare key, they found labelled in David's desk at Pear Tree Cottage.

When they arrived, he was scarcely conscious. Through directory enquiries they managed to arrange for a medic to call, who examined his wounds, which were pronounced superficial, gave him sedation, a sweet milky drink and advised them to call him again if David did not respond well.

By morning he was coming round. After a hearty breakfast they rustled up from the fridge, David haltingly briefed them on the situation binding them to secrecy on his suspicions about Desmond and Zac and the possible existence of deep treachery in the service.

'Emma, you must link with Professor James who is on the Board and explore the doubts about this whole tangled web.' He then fell fast asleep in Emma's arms who with Sara helped him back to bed. It was then that there was a knock on the door to the flat. They burst in spraying everyone with a stun-gun. When Emma and Sara came round David was gone. No note. Just gone.

David recognised his kidnappers some hours later when they splashed water in his face to revive him.

'Iqbal, Farhan, what are you up to? They were two of his agents recruited from Syria to assist in the vetting of migrants. Their task was to let friends of radical Islam through to continue the Caliph's battle against the apostates and pagans. Iqbal was brandishing a short sharp steel scimitar used for beheading. David's captors had been working for him as translators for the interrogation of refugees from the Middle East war zones who might be sleepers in ISIS cells. Fierce as his agents were, David was received well by an ISIS colonel, Assad, who believed David was working as a double agent, helping to filter ISIS members through the immigration checkpoints. Assad spoke quietly to David grasping his hand in brotherly friendship

'Allah be praised! You have done well for us. A curse on MI6 and all those apostate Christians. My brother we need you more than ever We want you to lead our new group planning the extension of ISIS cells across Europe and into North America via Quebec where French speaking terrorists from African states can be more readily inserted.

Keep on the inside track in London and pass on to us through the usual drop point all the information we need. Here are you tickets for London: you leave in the morning. Forgive the rough greeting. They thought you had been turned. '

David saw the whole scene was changing fast and wondered whether he could survive the crossfire of being so duplicitously engaged. He sipped his mint tea and crunched a chocolate ginger biscuit in his teeth, savouring the flavours on his tongue. He thought of Kendal mint cake on those treks across Westmoreland. Who was he with then on the hills decades ago. Yet the memories so sharp. He could remember the very rocks he marked

223

with his initials at last water and the steady pace of his steps as he followed the guide up the mountains. Where to go now with the clandestine book shop? That narrow interface between terrorists and freedom fighters, between loyalty and betrayal. Who were the goodies anymore, anyhow?

31. Mission Nova Scotia

Two days later David reappeared in London, to report to Desmond his escapades in Budapest and the risk of ISIS infiltration of the network. He was debriefed by Desmond and sent to Quebec to check reports that an ISIS cell was being set up there.

David was becoming increasingly uneasy about Sara and Emma though they were, he knew, safely back in Pear Tree Cottage. They had been told by Desmond that the palaver in Budapest was part of a complex hoax to provide better cover for David. A double exfiltration operation. Yet David had his continuing suspicions about the game Desmond was playing. After all these years, was he really still a friend or... And then there was the enigmatic Zac.

David had known Zac since his time at Dartmouth. Zac, or more formally Zachariah Owain Glyndwr, was from a small village in Rhosneig in Anglesey, Wales. His father, Isiah

Llywelyn Owain Glyndwr was a Welsh Wesleyan preacher and schoolmaster. Zac had been a brilliant student passing from the tiny chapel school on to secondary school. His father wanted for his son the best schooling and in Welsh, so, on from Ysgol Syr Thomas Jones secondary school, where he excelled in the sciences, thence to Bangor University, reading Science and Engineering, and for a master's in marine technology and naval architecture at The University of Plymouth, if David could remember correctly.

How David's once sharp faculty of instant recall of places and people and their stories was fading. But the intense memories of close encounters remained as vivid as the sun above the mast at noon. Zac had then moved to Dartmouth where he met David and they became close buddies. After the initial officer training, Zac had followed his science interests and specialised in professional naval engineering and communications technology. Never, however, had he lost his passion for the Welsh language, its culture and his fervent support for Welsh nationalism. He had a fine tenor voice and was a prize turn at mess parties, with operatic arias, popular songs, Welsh hymns and poetry and his finale the Welsh national anthem.

But lately Zac had become a mystery to David. His odd histrionics over the mock ISIS beheadings and the sudden appearance in Budapest before David's entrapment. David knew that Zac was now much chummier with Desmond and seemed to be quite enwrapped in the silence of the darkest secrets of the calling. No small talk about secret ops now, nor the latest weapons' research. David was quite out of the loop but he had heard mess talk that Zac was often off on briefing increments to safeguard key agents in the field in the far East and North Africa: but never a chat about that, as in the old times. Why? David wondered what was really up while he struggled to untie the tangled knots as he dozed on the flight to Canada.

In Quebec David was briefed on his new assignment as a triple agent, ostensibly supporting the newly set up ISIS cell under the cover of a health food shop, whilst his task for MI6 was to report on the plot, revealed in intercepted and decrypted signals, that ISIS was planning to assassinate the Canadian Prime Minister at a funeral service for an Israeli naval attaché to Quebec Province. The ISIS targets included Ivanka Chump and her husband, who have been working on the Palestinian accord and were personal friends of Jacob Gompertz, the deceased envoy. The funeral was to take place at sea on board the Royal Canadian Navy's Halifax class frigate Nova Scotia, the day after David's arrival.

The Canadians had been planning for the funeral service for some days. David was welcomed by the prime minister's aide de camp, Lieutenant François de la Haye, RCN. He briefed David on the protocol and David's formal role at the funeral which would take place off the coast near the Canadian naval base at Hastings.

David was introduced to Rear Admiral Scott King, head of the Canadian Forces

Intelligence Command (CFIC). King had received the signals from NATO about the alleged ISIS plot. David learnt that King was now liaising with Emile Bernard of the French Directorate for external security, who was due to arrive the next day. David recalled meeting him when Emile Bernard was French Ambassador in the UK.

It was at a cocktail at the French Embassy, a few years before, when David was surprised to learn that Bernard was quite fluent in Arabic after his time during the troubles in Algeria. They had shared some views on Arab culture and art with its ambiguous views on music, often greatly subdued under Islamic constraints, but vibrant in the local entertainment and north African cinema. They had talked about the new wave of cinema from the Maghrib countries, Algeria, Tunisia and Morocco which had fought to liberate the movies from the old-style Egyptian escapism of farce, melodrama and belly dancing, to focus on the social realities of modern life and to replace the stereotypes of suicide bomb terrorists and militant Islam, that audiences expected to see, with modern liberal Arab politics and religious practice of a younger generation of progressive thinkers. Yet now, David pondered, paradoxically, they were back in the thick of a new reality of militant ISIS, clandestinely deploying across all borders, to test the safe and the sacred places of the west and the waywardness of post-modern Muslim liberals. David was really enjoying his chat and wanted to meet Barnard again to seek his revised views on the risks facing North Africa after the suppression of the Arab Spring.

But David was cut short by the presentation of the funeral protocol and the associated security measures, which focused on the threat of mines being placed on the ship's hull and the continual screening of the keel with robotic search devices. David raised some questions in a separate security briefing on the screening of other shipping and the risk of attack by drones.

'Do not worry, my friend from Britain, these are anticipated and counter measures are fully in place. This is a first-rate modern upgraded frigate. As for other shipping, a twenty-mile exclusion zone had been established, with the exception of local inshore fishing sailing boats which generally appear before dawn and will be away out of the exclusion zone by the time of the funeral rites and the arrival by helicopter of the distinguished guests. Anyway, these sailing boats are all checked regularly by the coastguards with special attention to any suspicious activity in recent days.'

David still felt uneasy about the intelligence reports which were from reliable sources. He asked about the availability of other prevention and counter measures and personal protection of the ship's company and visitors. Had the lifeboat drill been practiced and were the anti-missile attack precautions in full readiness. Vice Admiral King reminded the security group, with heavy irony, that he well appreciated Commander Brand's concerns but what we are about is the practice of the solemn funeral rites for a late, beloved and distinguished foreign envoy and not the preparation of an armed assault exercise on one of the outer islands. Laying it on even thicker King, looking to the sky and rolling his eyes, reassured David that he personally would check the naval chaplain's cassock for any offensive weapons. He closed the meeting in a huff and marched off, muttering about arrogant British busybodies from naval intelligence, still treating the colonials as children.

David nodded, took a deep breath praying, softly, may Allah protect us all from ill-considered omissions of those in a few in high places. Commander Brand was now all the more determined to wear for the funeral his slim Navy Mark 3 inflatable life-jacket, with its LED light and a whistle, with an inflatable tag, all secured at the waist, over his dress uniform and under his Black cold-weather parka overcoat. It was this outfit that was to save his life.

32. Ghost ship

The next day, on board the Nova Scotia, at dawn, there was a high-level meeting with naval officers, diplomatic representatives and Jacob's father, a senior diplomat and former spy master from Mosad, the Israeli secret service. The funeral was planned to be conducted with full honours with a 21gun salute and burial at sea off the coast of Nova Scotia with wreaths of flowers strewn on the waters. David was familiar with the HMCS Nova Scotia. He remembered it had been in service for some years as a basic Halifax Class frigate, but had been extensively upgraded in an ANZC programme, along with frigates from other Commonwealth countries. All had been fitted with the latest Lockheed Aegis antimissile combat system, and torpedo defence capability. Nova Scotia had a top speed of 30 knots, from its General Electric gas turbine engine, carrying a complement of 225 officers and lower ranks, fully trained and experienced. They were all in that Halifax upgraded class now armed with Honeywell torpedoes, air missiles and a 57 mk3 Bofor gun. For logistical linkage Nova Scotia had a Sikorsky A CH 148 helicopter which could land aft, on a purpose-built pad. David thought, well-armed and well protected, it seemed, but were there weak points that ISIS knew how to exploit., he wondered. How would he disable such a frigate? Not that easy? Or was it…?

Meanwhile before midnight a small flotilla of ISIS fast Somali type pirate motor boats had captured a local thirty-foot clinker-built wooden fishing vessel, massacring the crew of five and arming it as a Ghost ship to attack the Frigate with shoulder held sea skimming Javelin missiles, aimed at the on-board helicopter and the Bofor gun. Ideally this would be timed as those attending the ceremony were performing the funeral rites and the gun salute. If the frigate was still making way, the sailing fishing boat, having technical priority of navigation, was planning to run across the bows of the frigate, causing the Nova Scotia to reduce speed and turn, exposing her broadside on. Then it would be attacked with the sea skimming Javelin missiles. The helicopter and the Bofor gun would be disabled and likely explode igniting their armaments. The funeral party would be machine gunned. In the confusion the fishing boat would ram the frigate's stern, dropping grenades to disable the rudder. The ISIS crew would use grappling hooks to scramble on board in a final act of suicidal explosions.

The plan of surprise attack in broad daylight worked nearly to perfection but with an added shock element. The naval and Quebec security services had deployed drones to check the area around the funeral, but they had been infiltrated by an ISIS sleeper technical agent, Ismut. He had been working as a member of the normal crew for two years and was well liked and friendly. But he was an ISIS warrior whose plan was to jam the Frigate's radio control systems, reprogramme the cameras of the drone robots and have them send back false images which would not betray the presence of the fishing vessel until it was within range of the javelin missiles.

After the dawn meeting, David saw a little fishing boat and wondered why it was not steering clear, but was on a path to cross the bows of the frigate risking a collision at sea. Technically it had right of way. He felt a surge of the Frigate's engines being roughly halted and slammed into reverse, the wheel being put hard to port, coming broadside on to the little sail boat. The coxswain sounded the deep throated horn and bawled a crude message on the loudspeaker.

Then the Frigate was attacked. The helicopter collapsed in flames, its armaments exploding. The Bofor gun became a tangle of steel on fire, its shell casings with blanks for the salute, going up in a whirl of flames. Then there was the machine gunning, the loss of steering and a sudden heaving of the whole ship as its main arsenal went up in smoke from a booby trap previously laid by the Ismut, the ISIS sleeper in the crew.

The radio and newspaper headlines 'ISIS sinks Canadian Navy frigate near Halifax – crew and VIPs attending VIP funeral on board massacred. PM orders Inquiry under top Judge. International outrage and extensive global multi media coverage condemned the attack. The ISIS assailants activated suicide vests; none recovered. The Inquiry was to focus on ISIS Somali links in planning.

A week later a body was hauled in by a charter fishing boat working out of Dingle Bay near Tralee in county Kerry on the west coast of Ireland. The decomposing corpse was in Royal Navy Lieutenant Commander's uniform, but strangely not wearing an inflatable life jacket. The charter fishing boat, which had expected a day's sport, hunting conger, ray and even blue shark, returned to port. The corps was put in a body bag by the local coast guard and transported to University Hospital in Kerry, where the on-call pathologist, Martin Greensmith was alerted.

33. Geoffrey James

Sara having moved on after her degree to post graduate research, was being supervised by Professor Geoffrey James. She was doing a project on comparative military security systems in the cyber age. She was having a tutorial with Professor James. She asked after her father having heard there was a spot of trouble in Budapest and later in Nova Scotia. James had heard that it was a burst gas main in Budapest and the frigate in Quebec had unaccountably hit a World War II mine that had drifted in from the Atlantic. Yet, these were mere cover stories that Melissa Olivier had put out as formal briefing at an Intelligence Security Committee meeting that James had attended as a special expert on computer-based cryptology. It was chaired by Dr Henry Williamson MP. He had been closely linked to work in this field since his time as an undercover agent subverting the attempted takeover of the

Labour Party by Militant, an extremist left wing group. He was well experience in sniffing out dire plots against the Establishment and the field work necessary for this. He retained an admirable scepticism about all claims by the top dogs and was deeply suspicious of Melissa and the manner of her rather fast rise to the top and her immediate entourage, including Professor Geoffrey James who seemed to him, just too smart to be true.

Later recognising Sara's concern, when he met her at the College coffee morning, Geoffrey invited her to tea at is family home in Cambridge; not that he was married but that's where he entertained his parents and his brother; moreover, for full measure he had a bright young post graduate Belgian student, Emile, as his informal housekeeper and partner.

Sara, wearing her usual grunge outfit, her bright green wig, arrived on her trendy orange Xuandong folding tricycle, with its small electric engine for uphill work; not that there was much call for that in the flat Cambridge environs. Sara removed her jade green crash helmet, hung it on her bike, pushed the door-bell and was greeted by Emile the houseboy, in his single leg white lycra running pants and black Dream Big long sleeve top. He smiled, breathed her name, brush kissed her on both cheeks, pervading her with his Hugo Boss fragrance, taking her gently by the hand and sweeping her into the minimalist lounge with its beanbag low cushions with a life-sized bronze sculpture of a prancing well-endowed prize bull. There was a Chinese gold lattice screen, standing on a huge double washed Chinese royal blue woollen fluffy rug, spread casually over a polished natural teak tiled floor and glistening in the evening sunlight slanting through the half closed golden venetian blinds. To Sara's surprise Emma was displaying herself in a swathe of multicoloured loose fitting veils, sipping a tall glass of fresh mint tea through a straw, amidst an aroma of Gabrielle Chanel perfume.

Geoffrey James put on a Mahler symphony at full amplification, drawing Emma and Sara into a corner, beyond the elaborate

240

Chinese screen, ostensibly to show them some porcelain he had brought back from the Far East. Geoffrey opened the conversation asking them what they had to tell him about David, assuring them that although he suspected the room has been bugged, they were safe behind the lead lined Chinese screen. They confided their suspicions of Desmond. They feared that David had been operating as triple master spy running double agents to unsettle ISIS and Taliban cells and to try to trap Desmond and Zac, whom he suspected of treachery and who might be controlled by a more senior person within HQ. Geoffrey James, shuffled his feet, called to Emile to serve the tea and cakes and quickly turned the conversation around as if he were concealing something from them.

Emile reappeared with a tray of goodies, cress and egg sandwiches, a variety of delicious salty pastries, a splendid array of more glasses of fresh mint tea, smoked trout with a light lemon sauce on pita bread, followed by strawberry trifle from locally harvested fresh fruit. After Emma and Sara had left together, thanking Geoffrey for the entertainment, they were each rewarded, by Emile, at the front door, with a soft hand on the arm and Hugo Boss perfumed kisses on both cheeks.

Then, Emma had a riotous ride with Sara through the backstreets of town chattering twenty to the dozen and hooting with joyful laughter about the sinuous ministrations of the Belgian house-boy, with satirical guesses at the subject of his post-graduate research and the modish one long legged lycra hotpants, which had the effect of him seemingly jealously competing with the more overt endowments of the prize bronze bull.

Geoffrey James caught the next train to town having arranged an urgent meeting with Melissa Olivier, Head of MI6. He briefed her on the encounter with Sara and Emma. Melissa advised James that she had had Desmond under close surveillance and had also suspicions of Zac. They, she feared, had together too readily gone along with a plan to silence David. But she needed hard evidence of treachery before she could act. She asked James to lead a confidential

242

enquiry into them both, after checking again the credentials of their security ratings. Melissa laughed to herself.

'Never straightforward.'

She turned back to her coffee that was getting cold. Then that nasty suspicion.

'Even an innocent cup of coffee: but surely not here from her own percolator; her own staff?'

She mused,

'I wonder how our protégée, is faring under dear Emma's care? Sharp as a rapier, they say at the interview at Russell. Must see that CCTV footage again. And perhaps put a tail on her and on Maryam. Can't be too careful with these double agents. Never like the idea myself. Distasteful and unreliable.'

She looked at her diary.

'Must get another manicure and pedicure. Having that review next week with MinCom. Cecil will be in the chair. Never keeps his hands to himself. Can't disappoint him. He well knows the games I have had to play and just wants to have a free go. Rascal!'

'Let's fit Miss Brand in. Give her a check.'

Later

Melissa briefed herself on the reports on Sara on the file.

'After being senior cryptologist... startling advance. Double first and working on R&D parttime...'

There was a knock on the door.

'Come!'

Sara strode in, bowed her head slightly.

'Morning ma'am, you asked to see me.'

'Yes, indeed Miss Brand. Thankyou Timothy, that will be all. Do take a seat.'

They moved to the sofa area, for informal chats. Her assistant closed the door quietly and turned on the speaker linked to the microphone, concealed in the flowers on the coffee table.

'It's good to see you again. I am delighted with your rapid progress. The reports I have seen are glowing. I am so glad you have been able to make friends and master everything so well, despite the problems you must have had over your father's difficulties.'

244

'Yes, Ma'am, all very disturbing, but my step-mother and my father's sister have been a great support in this sad time. ISIS are so brutal.'

'Yes, indeed. But your father nailed the killer...'

'You must know, Miss Brand, your father was one of our best and most respected senior staff members. We want you to follow up on his work. We want you to penetrate into the information systems ISIS have, to track down the links they have with the Taliban and with international trade and commerce. You will be assigned to narrow down the field of suspects, through your skills in IT surveillance and cryptology.'

'Is there a protocol for this role.'

'No, so you must develop one. You can work with Josef Lukulescu who is over here from Langley. He has been working on this kind of operation for a decade, screening the migrants from South America and the students from China. '

'Thankyou Ma'am, is that all?'

245

'Yes, Miss Brand, but keep me briefed on progress. My door is always open, just check first with Timothy.'

Professor Geoffrey James returned to Cambridge on the next train from London, oblivious that Frank Trueman, a wolf in sheep's clothing, under an FCO Ministerial initiative, was closing in on the bunch of them, Melissa included. Emile had been infiltrated into James' household some months before and was a solid source of hot intelligence behind his bizarre façade.

34. The Pathologist

He had just arrived in post that week, doing routine hospital autopsies on mainly elderly people crippled with stroke or end stage cancer or renal failure after years of chronic diabetes and no available transplant service. Then this. A washed-up body flown from County Kerry Killarney by the Admiralty. In full naval uniform, with a note from the University Hospital Kerry, 'Over to you chum, Martin Greensmith.' He unzipped the body bag noting in his report book burn marks on the head and some shrapnel on the hands.

Bryan Summerfield was new to forensic pathology, he had been qualified at the Cambridge Institute of Criminology under one of the leading world specialists in the field, Professor Joshua Sherman, but was something of a debutant at the practice with just three years' experience. The Police who had delivered the body had left some identification and other documents found in the pockets of the naval uniform.

David Brand RN born 27 July 1970, 6ft 2 inches tall, Sandy hair, blue eyes, scar on left cheek, Service number and a telephone number of a Ministry of Defence unit, various pocket litter including house keys, a wallet with £253 in notes and coin, a two days' old supermarket receipt, various debit and credit cards, a photo of a young girl and a mace spray. Bryan phoned the Ministry of Defence number and asked for the medical records' department.

'Burnside here.'

'Harold?'

'Yes Harold Burnside.'

'Bryan Summerfield here, the Cambridge Institute. You may remember me from the Cambridge Institute course you were on.'

'Indeed, your brilliant seminar on doubtful suicides.'

'Yes, well I need your advice and help on a case before me now. I'm at the Institute of Naval Medicine at Gosport now, where we specialise in drowning incidents. Have a case, a naval officer, seemed straight forward enough at first, but I've hit a snag. I just wonder if you have any records on the man I am examining.'

He quoted the identification details including the date of birth.

'Well, Bryan, you may be in luck we do have on-line here digital records as far back as January 1970, so we may be able to help right now, and I could indeed tell you what we have. Let me see David Brand date of birth 27 07 1970. Hold on, yes, yes indeed we have some data here. Let me tell you...'

'Does it say a scar on the right cheek?'

'No! But it states a scar on the left cheek.'

'Sorry, that's not correct, as on the identification papers we have here. But strange thing is, this body has no scar on either cheek. What about the hair colour, sandy?

'Yes, that's correct with a full set of beard and moustache.'

'Hmm...Stranger still: this guy is virtually bald!'

'Do you want any more, like blue eyes, part of lobe of right ear missing, small finger of left hand truncated'.

'No, chum that's enough, seems to be an error somewhere on the line.'

Bryan thanked Harold profusely and returned to the autopsy room. He unzipped the body again and looked more closely at the face to check for scars and the earlobe injury. Nothing. He felt the face carefully along the chin line, pulled and he found in his hands a complete face mask and beneath a face older and more deteriorated than a two-day old corpse would be, close shaven with no naval full set.

Bryan Summerfield left the autopsy room again. Picked up the phone and dialled the police who had brought in the body. As he did so a softly spoken man took the receiver from his hand and replaced it on the phone rest.

'Bryan, be a good boy and just certify the stiff as dead from drowning and let us have your succinct report, and we shall cause you no bother.'

'But...'

'Bryan, we really do not want to be a trouble to you and your nice family. Keep this all secret between the two of us, there's a good lad and we will put in a good word for you with your boss.'

'But I can't sign this, it's just not the right man and it is all very strange, the coroner should be informed…'

'Not today Bryan, or else…'

'Or else what?

'Well, Bryan, would your Julia, like to see those rather frank photos of you with dear Sophie from the Ayurvedic spa… We all have secrets. Let's be sensible.'

The soft-spoken man showed Bryan his card from MI6. Bryan returned to the autopsy room where he found that his assistant, had undressed the corpse and had begun to take some X-rays to check for broken bones. Bryan mused, could be Jewish or Muslim, odd that.

The soft voice followed him.

Bryan coldly turned to him.

'Not in here please, unless you are fully gowned. Infection risks. Please get out, I will see what I can do to meet your needs.'

35. Sara's revenge

Sara learned that her father seemingly has been assassinated and there could be a contract out for her life. After his funeral at which only one lowly Friend from MI6 attended, she visited at night the mausoleum where her father's body was placed, contemplating suicide.

Sara breathing deeply took out a pill sewn into the lining of her dress, believing it to be a fatal dose. She eyed the pill and placed it carefully on the stone slab beside her where she was sitting, trembling. She reflected back on her short, troubled life and all its pain and promise. She sighed.

'What a waste!'

As daylight flickered through the highest stained-glass panes, she sensed she was not alone and tried to wrestle with her mind not sure if was a nightmare or that she had taken the pill and passed on. Sara felt for the pill. It had indeed gone. Her hands trembled in the cold and with the awesome action she had taken. She shivered as the cold rose to her knees. She sensed there was a strange cramped image beside her, silent, dressed in white with gleaming teeth, illuminated in blue and gold by the slanting rays through the stained glass. The upper face of the creature was in shadow.

'Lucifer?' Sara gasped and muttered,

'Have I come her to die...'

'No, Sara you came here yesterday!'

'Are you Moloch, to take me to Lucifer and down to Hell's fire.'

'No, I am Trueman, we have met before.'

Sara opened one eye and saw the cramped character in white was in a wheel chair and smiling.

'But the pill, I'm surely dead now and so cold!'

Trueman opened his right hand. The pill was there.

'My dear Sara pills like that went out long ago, maybe it was Temazepam (Restoril) or even a vitamin cocktail of calcium, magnesium and zinc. Was it from your father? An old service joke among friends?'

Sara was feeling dizzy and thought she would faint, or vomit.

'Maybe even morphine as a relief from expected torture...'

Sara threw up and collapsed on the floor sobbing. Trueman , pocketed the pill and grasped her hand.

'The poison pill gag is now preserved only in spy thrillers. Here, have some water. And don't be afraid of me: you're in safe hands, with someone paralysed from the waist down. I'm just your babysitter'

'OMG, I'm still here. So, fetch Taylor Swift!'

'No, it's true, by the way, that is not your father in the tomb. He survived the ISIS strike on HMCS frigate Nova Scotia off the coast of Halifax. And he is now working again under a new identity, as Dick Barnes. Mum's the word, we must keep our heads down, the world is not what it seems.'

'Can I contact Dad?'

'Beyond the grave, the undiscovered country? Maybe: not yet. It's not finished. We linger on, as ever, at the interface between truth and our deceptive grasp of it. Let it unfold, my dear. Patience is a critical quality among friends.'

'Frank! Can I trust you?'

'Trust? A tricky word these days.'

'Revenge is what I need now. Who is it? ISIS? Really. Or an inside job, reaching right to the top?'

'Revenge may come. But not now. Let's get you home to Maryam, who is distraught.'

I have my buggy outside if you can give me a push. But mind you, no Salsa, now.'

'No Frank, it's past midnight after all!'

Yet, Sara had an odd feeling about the whole show especially Geoffrey James, as if he were hiding something. And as Frank dropped her off at Emma's place, he pressed a soft kiss to her cheek.

Sara slept in Emma's arms, sobbing. Then after a light lunch on the lawn she slept again. And as the evening drew in, she turned to Emma.

'Can we really trust him, dearest Emma?

'Frank?'

'No, not Frank, he's solid. You know jolly Geoffrey James, my prof and mentor.'

Emma smiled.

'You mean, he's an odd ball?'

Sara suppressed a giggle.

'Can't be sure what's worn under the kilt, can we?'

Emma scoffed,

'That he's bad 'tis pity and pity 'tis, 'tis true!

'Indeed Sara. One can surmise thus from his houseboy...'

'The Belgian, Emile?'

'All looks, and I sensed from his fragrance, rather queer.'

'But we should not hold that against him these days. No. But decidedly odd. And ill advised, could turn against him in a gangplank pitch.'

'Blackmail.'

'For sure. We must all be on our guard.'

'Guard thine honour!'

'Oh, dear Emma, surely not at risk with such as Geoffrey James, or even the bulging Emile.'

256

'Darling Sara, you are right on the ball, excuse the expression.'

More joyous giggles.

'Give no-one your trust, you mean?'

'Not even yourself. Beware darling Sara, you may be fated to be your own worst enemy.'

36.   David betrayed

It was in the ambush by the Ghost ship, that the Canadian frigate Nova Scotia, was mortally damaged from external missiles, from machine gunning and from bombs planted in the engine room within. She slowly foundered and slipped below the waves, carrying with her all aboard in her battered hulk to the depths of the cold Atlantic Ocean with little trace, save for some scattered ship's fittings, the acrid smell of oil, and decaying human debris left floating on the surface attracting scavenging birds. So little to show of the elegant frigate, where it had shortly been dressed all over in mourning for the death of a distinguished foreign diplomat.

So, soon all was washed away, save for a few floating body parts of corpses and clinking pots and pans and tattered flags and drapes and a lone black biretta hat that had been solemnly worn by the officiating priest in his frock dress, lawn sleeves, surplice, and carrying his pastoral staff and order of service. Now, all but his biretta gone.

Rescue boats were quickly there and helicopters from Hastings, searching for any sign of life or critical debris of the once proud ship.

'Ahoy!' a plaintive sailor's cry from the captain's pinnace launched from the sister frigate, Ontario, that had been amongst the first of the recue craft on the scene, steaming in at its top pace of some 30 knots. The pinnace circled closer to a mass of floating debris from which there appeared a faint light, that the young sailor had spotted. The accumulated flotsam adhering to the mass was untangled with a boathook in the excited hands of ordinary seaman Jock Macarthy, straight out of training. As he separated the remnants and located the source of the light he revealed a body, still breathing and a hand moving slightly and an eye opening and mouth stuttering.

'Ahoy there, matelot! It was David in his Navy Mark 3 life jacket with its automatic indicator LED light. They took him on board the pinnace, wrapped him in a Mylar rescue blanket against the elements, and then transferred him to the frigate Ontario, where he was identified from the documents he was carrying. They revived him with hot cocoa before he was rapidly airlifted by helicopter to the naval medical centre in Hastings. David was put in a warm room, stripped of his wet clothing, which was placed on a bedside locker. He was then wrapped in fluffy. dry woollen blankets, put in a warm bed and fed with hot drinking chocolate as, he slowly recovered from his shock and hypothermia. He slept soundly.

Meanwhile the Canadian secret service had been alerted. They tipped off MI6. They activated a local asset, a British agent, Carlos Lopez, covertly working as an orderly in the medical centre. He crept into David's room. He approached the bedside locker, just catching the mug with the remnants of the drinking chocolate, as it nearly fell to the marble floor. Lopez located the drenched naval suit David had been wearing. He carefully searched the pockets, removing all the sodden contents

David was carrying, placing them in a zipped plastic bag. Then Lopez substituted a set of freshly forged, salty wet documents, into David's uniform pockets and a packet of carefully selected salty-water pocket litter. This included various local shop receipts, a cinema ticket stub, a leather wallet with British and Canadian currency, a photo of a young woman on a bicycle and a forged debit card, all having been available as the agent's stock-in -trade, and updated, should such a need arise. Lopez also inserted into an inner breast pocket of David's clothes a sheaf of forged encrypted documents downloaded from London, to seal David's fate.

Lopez had been well trained and well paid as a sleeper for the past two years after he had migrated from Spain. The next day Lopez passed on the originals from David's clothes for his controller to collect in a designated dead drop behind a mirror in the medical centre canteen washroom. Lopez signalled the drop when cycling from the centre at midday wearing a Real Madrid supporters' cap. He remained an avid La Liga football fan, following their matches on Sky Sports.

Later that evening, at the Hastings medical centre, there was a preliminary medical assessment and much interchange with MI6 in London and with the local police services. Then David still recovering from his ordeal, was roughly awoken from his sleep, arrested by a Canadian police sergeant, body searched and under armed escort flung into the military prison at Hastings naval yard, awaiting trial for espionage. For, he had been found carrying in his sea-soaked uniform encrypted messages and other documents showing his apparent clandestine links as an ISIS agent implicated in crooked dealing with the Taliban over heroin smuggling. His passport in the name of Commander Albert Karl Bernhard and all his other belongings were confiscated including the photo of the young girl on a bicycle. David was then tranquilised and given a sleeping draught against his will. As he passed out, crying himself to sleep, his drifting thoughts were for the warm embrace of Maryam and the smiling face of his brilliant daughter Sara.

Under Melissa's instructions, Geoffrey James was immediately flown over ostensibly to interrogate the prisoner. He calmed David down, who had now revived and snarling with anger. James explained the new plan to David and called the head of the Canadian Secret Service, who agreed to his terms. A pliant medical officer was found who signed a certificate of death by drowning of Commander Albert Karl Bernhard. Then after preliminary enquiries, Geoffrey James asserted, they had failed to find any of Bernhard's living relatives and called for a cremation to be arranged. The readily accommodating medic signed up for the cremation, pocketing a fee somewhat larger than his normal practice. James had David's drinking chocolate quietly drugged and with an escort he removed David slumped in a wheel chair from the Hastings medical centre and transferred him a safe house. Later James called Melissa Olivier. 'Job done'

Melissa recorded in her official report that David was a now deceased double agent formerly working for ISIS. She told James to abandon his investigation into Desmond and Zac, as suspicions over them could now be ignored, at least for a while. James mused that there must be another fate that she had in store for them.

Melissa issued James with detailed instructions on the next steps with David and the need for a body double to be dropped off near the west coast of IIreland. She added that the double should be preferably already recently dead, from drowning, and if not, James should make appropriate arrangements. James questioned whether it was not all getting rather too intricate.

'Why go to the extremes of killing off Bernhard and then slipping a body double of David to the coast of Ireland with David sent back by plane under another guise? Melissa getting exasperated with James told him those were his orders and just get on with it.

Melissa, was determined to humiliate Brand who could no longer be trusted after his defection to ISIS. She also had a hunch he was on to her over the Taliban deal. She never was keen on triple agents. They never worked well and were likely to be the targets of opposing forces. Neither side could fully trust them. David could not just be dismissed from the Service: he knew too much. She would have to have him back and then quietly dispose of him and his unreliable family after a thorough interrogation, probably under the current extraordinary rendition scheme with enhanced interrogation, maybe in Iraq in Abu Ghraih prison or at the Bagram Airforce base in Afghanistan, which had worked so well in the past. The usual airports in Wales or Scotland could not be used for secret rendition.

'Converted to Islam indeed! That is just not in the rule book. Could get quite out of control like the history of the East India Company and the marriages of senior staff to Muslim princesses.'

'No! James must obey orders. And maybe he needed to be tailed. A little honey pot diversion might do the trick with him. Men are so susceptible. Wasn't there a young French maid, Anne-Marie, on the staff at Russell College who had helped in the past with the College Master to get him in line?'

Melissa made a note. She also decided to deepen the subterfuge by calling Desmond and brief him on the turn of events. She would tell him her plan for a new cover story that David had confessed to his guilt before he sadly expired at Bagram. Moreover, he had revealed after further interrogation, that he held no longer any suspicions about Desmond's alleged treasonous activities with Zac. Melissa smiled as she wove a web that could entrap them all and ensure her escape to Guyana with the Taliban millions. She would retire there under the spell of those charming, young, and thrillingly vigorous beach boys.

Melissa then signalled Desmond and Zac to stand by ready for further instructions about David and the fate of Maryam and Sara who might have been part of the conspiracy against the HQ senior staff. She kept to herself that there was some intelligence from the Taliban in Kabul that she, herself, was on a Foreign Office list of suspected double agents. So, before the net tightened speed was essential. She sniffed up a little of the white powder she kept for special occasions. She had to confess that such occasions were now becoming more frequent.

Putting the phone down Desmond poured himself a large gin and tonic and pumped his fists exhilarated that the whole worry over the David issue, was now melting away.

James, in Hastings, checked his notes on the detailed instructions from Melissa. There was clearly much to be done. He set about getting a team together of local agents along with Carlos Lopez and activated the local financial support account. He mused that the well-established practice, dating back half a century or more, of opening bank accounts with forged sterling paper, remained the principal means of oiling the wheels and the pockets of the full-time officers, of other assets and their contacts in the field.

James first proceeded with the body double task, setting up what he saw as an Operation Mincemeat in reverse. This time not to fool the enemy but to trick our own emergency services and to have a little added amusement in alerting the Irish Garda with a false body double and planted forged secret papers about a threatened ISIS plot to blow up the Post Office in Dublin. If his contacts in the pathology department at the medical centre failed, then a clandestine kidnapping would do, of a suitable Hobo from the many homeless around Hastings, or from the near defunct railway system sleeper. If the worst came to the worst there was a regular supply of drunken sailors on Saturday nights from the naval centre on Cape Breton Island. The navy would not miss one immediately: they would just write it down as a bit of AWOL at least until Monday morning. James was sure the local well-groomed Service team would fix it somehow.

Then he had to get a submarine diverted from the Clyde for dropping the stiff off the coast of Killarney. No doubt the local Garda would be on to the job. They, as from any loyal EU country, would be seriously worried about the proposed ISIS plot on the famous ancient Post Office in Dublin, evident in the planted documents that they could decode by virtue of the EU cryptology links.

James thought, 'What a boon it is for them to be seen as dutiful members of the EU. Brand's defection, treachery and well-deserved demise would be headlines across Intelligence services from Dublin to Tallin, from Lisbon to Copenhagen. Brand would become a non-person, and his family under a deep cloud of suspicion.'

James pondered, 'All do-able with a bit of luck, I guess. But then what is my destiny? Professor at a distinguished and well supported Cambridge College, devoted well reimbursed servant of the secret service. And then…' The more he pondered the more he was in doubt.

'Is Melissa entirely Kosher? And that strange child Sara. Perky, brilliantly clever, and getting so close to that cripple Frank Trueman at the ball? Never really had his measure. Checked his background. Clean as a whistle. Yet suspiciously so. Nothing on his file. But then Turing was the same and of course Philby and his lot. Fooled everyone, even the top brass and ministers. Rotten luck, for Frank Trueman with such terrible war wounds. But then...?'

Geoffrey James suddenly caught his image from the glass panels of a book case, looking louche. He had often wrestled with his personal dilemma for trying to keep his strictly academic duties and pride in his cryptology, admired on the international circuit, separate from his covert operations with Melissa, whom he despised, but had become her acolyte. What was to be his destiny? An international celebrated academic, assisting a fine intelligence community out of sheer patriotism: or a forlorn dead-duck despised in academia and sunk in the squalid trade of Melissa's corrupted ways of espionage. The problem was he was now in it up to his neck and lacked the courage to steal away from it all. His once high ideals he had been already forsaken. To fall on his sword, increasingly attracted his conscience. But was he man enough for that?

So, finally, David would be fitted out with new togs and documents and would be secretly repatriated under a new cover as Dick Barnes, only to meet the fate that dear Melissa was arranging for him and his little family. Then there was the mask maker. A cast from David's face would have to be arranged, through Geoffrey James' contacts with the Neptune theatre in Halifax. Next, he must recover David's uniform from the medical centre. Lopez could readily do that, replacing the original papers and waiting to fit-up the dead body double.'

Desmond called Zac who both celebrated quietly, Zac watching his favourite video of Wales beating England again at Twickenham and Desmond knocking back his favourite Irish Whiskey.

Melissa Oliver was at Brown's boutique hotel in Knightsbridge, in the shower room with the water running at full blast, to distract any listening devices. She signalled Geoffrey James on her encrypted smart phone to arrange papers for David to be covertly sent back to London by the earliest plane and for him to be given two week's leave to recuperate under a new identity. She could then decide on the next steps to obliterate her tracks over the Taliban deal and to suitably dispose of the doubters and non-starters for the next phase.

She turned off the shower, arranged loosely around her shapely figure a semi-transparent negligée slipping under the bed covers where she has been taking a break from sleeping with the insatiable General Qadim Shah Yaftali, head of Afghan Intelligence Services' Kandahar office. Qadim was on a diplomatic assignment at the Embassy in Kensington. Melissa had extracted all she needed from her lover and slipped him a list of British agents in Kabul together with the names and contact details of her good treacherous friends, Desmond and Zac.

To be frank though, Melissa found herself tiring of Serge's persistent ministrations. She mused that the Taliban could be given a free hand, for a hefty sack of the dried milky sap extracted from a trawl of the new harvest of Papaver Somniferum poppy seeds. That would be a cheap price for the contact details and their engagement to take out the superfluous non-starters Desmond and Zac, now that she was arranging for Brand to be liquidated. She turned again to mount Qadim, smiling at him with her green tinted eyes, shooting him dead in the heart, with her Glock 17 pistol, which she carried in a thigh holster concealed under her negligée.

She left the pistol on the bed, returned to the shower to freshen up, knowing that Qadim's body would be retrieved by his deputy Khan Sharif Karimi, listening via the bug tuned to the adjacent suite. Karimi checked the drugged, bound and gagged body of a local kidnapped Egyptian student he had beside him in his room. He had the signal from Melissa to complete the job.

Karimi had been eagerly awaiting this moment when his malicious, narcissistic chief, Qadim, would be set aside. Promotion would automatically follow and armed with the list of British agents and the contact details of Melissa Olivier's non-starters, Karimi would be the toast of Kabul. He would be also forearmed not to submit again to the palpable but deadly charms of Melissa's honey pot team. Though he had often enjoyed the gentle touches of Ursula after a vigorous session in the Battersea VIP sports' gym.   Maybe just once more before he took his plane home. It would be a pity not to say goodbye to the generous curves of Ursula.

But, first, he must drag the unconscious student from Cairo in the next room, through the linked door. Then after he was done, he would be free to have that farewell romp. He awaited Melissa's discreet departure, dragged the supine student into the adjacent room where Qadim's body lay in bed in a pool of blood, his mouth still open in surprise, or was it in rapture? He opened Qadim's over-night bag, took out his M9 Biretta pistol with its silencer. He loaded it, shooting the drugged student in the forehead. He then interlinked the two bodies on the bed and placed Melissa's Glock 17 in

Qarim's fist. He departed softly closing the bedroom door behind him, thinking only of Ursula's charms, not knowing this was to be his last day in London alive. He was fished out the Thames, two days later, apparently drowned when drunk, probably falling from the parapet of one of the many London bridges over the Thames that in its history, had washed up so many bodies with the incoming tide, riffling them against the locks at Teddington.

A week later at Russell College: High table dinner. Geoffrey James revealed to Sara the terrible news of David's death and defection and asked her to go to Kabul to join a section infiltrated into Afghan Intelligence services. She could do this under cover of her research project. He also told her of Serge's death involved with Melissa in dubious circumstances in which a visiting student from Egypt and Qadim had been found dead in what seemed to be a suicide pact in a hotel. Melissa had survived: the student was dead. Sara heard all this from James, as the vintage port was served.

Yet, Sara could not believe in David's treachery and suspected Melissa and James may be traitors. She determined to unravel the mystery surrounding Desmond and Zac and the strange case of Albert Bernhard that she had found in a briefing note on the Nova Scotia affair she had hacked that morning.

Next day Sara returned south. As she pondered on the entangled strands of the story over supper with Maryam, at Pear Tree Cottage, she had a call from London by a senior staff officer Major John George, to proceed to MI6 HQ on the next train for a briefing for her planned Afghan trip. But she hesitated and after a debate with Maryam they agreed Sara should first, link up with Frank, whom they both trusted, to check out what was really going on. She fixed an early meeting with Frank Trueman at Waterloo station. Tally Ho!

37. Waterloo Bridge

Frank Trueman found Sara wating under the big clock at Waterloo station. He greeted her warmly in his wheelchair. They left together to find his parked disability adapted Ford Mustang. He drove her along the bridge over the Thames. The engine on the Mustang, was subdued to a walking pace, growled quietly under the restraint of third gear, as seagulls flew noisily overhead and the salt water breeze wafted over them on the rising tide. Sara smiled across as he kept the sportscar in check with just hand controls. She touched his shoulder. He smiled and whispered to her, 'Sara, I need to warn you about…'

Frank's mobile vibrated.

'Trueman.'

'Banyan here, Langley.'

'You! How can I help, good friend?

'We have a problem, with your problem, brother.'

'How come?'

'Presidential cock-up. Have to take a rain check.'

'You can't be serious; we need your local people now.'

'No go, brother, all tied up.'

'You see the big issue is that President Diamond Chump, can you believe it? He's Goddamn refused to accept election defeat. OMG, he's now declared a state of emergency. The White House and the Capitol are blockaded by US Army troops loyal to Chump. Colonel Stormy Rachel Whirlwind (she's called Breezy, you know after that well shaped drifter in a Clint Eastward movie). Well Breezy, with plenty of her chest candy to the fore declares martial law over the entire Federal Capital, of Washington D.C. And then sequests the Supreme Court, putting all them judges, John Roberts and all, into isolation. She then jams the public internet and social media. Meanwhile the newly elected President Bjorn Hayden, yet to be confirmed, calls out the National Guard and the Special State Operations Command to them Boogaloo boys for Chump to tell 'em to drop their weapons. SOCOM responds Molon Labe, their motto. Then Hayden orders the Constitutional procedures to be continued for his confirmation in the IMF building, downtown. Then, SOCOM quell the rioters on both sides. Hayden then, would you believe it, orders the National Guard Commander Hogan Brice to oust Whirlwind. The Pentagon is destabilised awaiting developments and the CIA confined to barracks. OMG it's just a soup sandwich here. 'It's a TARFU, political and military deadlock, here brother. Stale mate. No way we can help with your troubles. You could try NATO.

Oh! Are you still there?'

'A-OK!'

'And, Trueman, watch out for those rogue elements in the Taliban in Kabul. They are into selling tonnes of poppy seed through the back channels. We hear that your top office is deep into this shit. Not sure to what end. Keep an eye on the top bitch. Some hanky-panky: our assets talk of a Guyana connection…'

The special line fell silent.

279

Sara turned to Frank Trueman.

'What's up?'

'Oh! That. Yep, Some little political punch-up in Washington. Not to worry we can use other channels. I have some NATO mates. I'll call them up. But we must watch our backs: some dirty work at the crossroads in the heroin trade. They may guess we are on to them, so you should decline to go on the Afghan assignment. Plead illness.'

Frank left Sara at Charing Cross Station on the Strand, slipping into her hand a pen-drive. 'Play this, my dear, and then delete it all. It's your fathers debriefing at MI6, copied from the master record. There is a contract out for his life. You and Maryam may well be the next. Melissa and her cronies, including Prof. James are crooked and suspect you are on to it. Take good care little sprite!' And he then sped off towards Whitehall.

38.   Charing Cross

Sara, deeply shocked by her encounter with Frank, plugged the pen-drive, Frank had given her, into her smart phone and started listening to David's debriefing at MI6. It was a terrifying record of duplicity. For after the interrogation had finished and David had left the room the microphone had been left on revealing the depth of treachery at the top of MI6, involving both Melissa and all the more shocking to Sara, Professor Geoffrey James, whom she had at first, so trusted.

Her tears flowed as she realised the horrific future unfolding for her father, Maryam and herself.

'Are you alright dear? You look all in.'
A passing woman, in sunglasses and wearing a knitted shawl over her long skirted woollen dress, with the scent of lavender about her, enquired and put her hand on Sara's arm.

'Can I get you a coffee or something? You don't look at all well, my dear.'

'No really, I'm Ok. Just had a bit of a shock. Really, I'll be fine in a minute. Thank you for your concern.'

'Had some bad news on your mobile. Same as me last year. Heard my mother had died. Not easy to get over that. Sure you are OK? Pluck up your courage. Life can be a real bugger!'

Sara smiled.

'Thank you so much. I'll be OK. Yes, a bit of a shock.'

'Sure. We all get over it after a while. I try to think of the good times we had together. Look on the bright side, I always say. Look, my dear, the sun is coming out for you.'

The woman moved away taking the scent of lavender with her. Sara looked hard at the pen-drive and deleted the file. She filched in her bag, for a paper handkerchief, but found she was touching the friendly warm leather spine of her diary. She sniffed. Pulling out the keep-sake she started to write down her thoughts jumbled as they were.

Extract from Sara's diary;

Just listened to Frank's pen-drive. OMG, what another omnishambles. All deleted now. But we're all for the chop. Melissa, Desmond, Zac and even James in it up to their necks.... AMIRITE?

Frank's such a fam makes me glowup when I see him. Really woke and a bit of a snack too. TBH I'M L without him. Finna cringe for a week from that pen-drive stuff.

Grilled Dad so hot. Told them all about the fake master plan for overthrowing the West. They probably took it for real. I'm a baby. Yikes low key. Zac and Des real sus and tools for Melissa who's a top cap.

Sara then thought the diary entry was naïve and dangerous. She had better be careful. In the wrong hands... She would have to warn Myriam and David asap. She walked across the bridge to the Southbank, passing the Eye and the Festival Hall and onto Waterloo, glimpsing the shell inspired waterfall outside the Shell building. She thought, strange how it never had water flowing from it. Must be problems with spray as that passageway was very gusty.

She reached Waterloo station taking a train down to Francisfield. She was trembling uncontrollably as she walked up to Lower Sheer where Pear Tree Cottage lay so tranquil, the sweet smell of honeysuckle pervading the air and the martins making their nests under the eaves, with not a care in the world. Sara's mind was in turmoil and she felt sick in the pit of her stomach. Tears formed in her eyes as she feared her world was about to implode and her much loved father and dear Maryam, who had become a fresh loving mother to her, were about to be lost. Her eagerness for that transition from girl to woman was fast becoming a nightmare.

39. Prince Albert taken

'Ma'am, it's Sir Samuel Cecil on the line, shall I put him through?'

'Who? Natasha, who?'

'Samuel Cecil from the Royal Protection Service for the Prince of Wales, Prince James. Says it's urgent and Top Secret. If you will take it, I will put on the Royal Scrambler'

'OK. Put him through...Good morning, Sir Samuel, Melissa Olivier here. How can I help?'

'Fraid it's a bit of a crisis. It's Prince Albert...Bertie

'Prince James's son?'

'Exactly. He's been taken!'

'Taken?'

'Yes Ma'am. Prince Albert, James's son, third in-line to the throne, has been taken. (Unintelligible screech.}

'Could you repeat that. The line's not too good today, with the Royal scrambler on...'

(Another faint voice with a strong Estuary accent)

'Bob! You on it, mate? Clear the bloody line. It's the fucking palace on to Melissa. Sharp to it lad, she'll be getting' her knickers in a twist.'

(More screeching and sound of levers being thrown.)

(Another voice; a woman with Yorkshire burr.)

'So, Mabel, I were waiting while the bus, and he cums oop, so close, yer know, I could feel his hot breath down me neck and he were pressing hiself gainst me bum...'

'Bob! Come on mate, it's the red switch on the right. Seems you found Dolores in the kitchen. Pull your fucking finger out or Melissa will 'ave us for breakfast...'

'Sod it Jim, it's the new system. Should be A1 now. Testing. All systems going.'

'So sorry, Sir Samuel, we seem to have had a crossed line somewhere. We are having a new server installed, technical bods all over the place. We seem to be clear now. Please confirm.'

'Melissa, it's Samuel Cecil still here. But call me back on the secure line just to be sure.'

'Natasha, you still there?

'Yes Ma'am.'

'Get Sir Samuel back on the line. Check the security clearance before you put him through. And make a note, I want to see those technical bods, Jim and Bob at 2pm sharp and tell them I want a full report and all the checks to be made. Oh, Natasha, were you listening in?

'Yes, Ma'am and taking notes, as back up for the recording system.'

'Well, Natasha, let's leave it at Jim and Bob whoever they are. We can overlook dear Mabel and Dolores with their little excitement for the day. The risks of public transport for young girls these days.'

'Not so young, Ma'am, but they play the field, if you know what I mean.'

'Outside office hours is not our concern, Natasha. But it seems boys are still being boys at bus stops.'

'I'm putting him through again Ma'am. All systems checked on the secure link…

(Faint clicking sounds)

'You are through Sir Samuel, Dame Melissa Olivier on the line now.'

'Melissa, whatever happened. Just went dead this end.'

'No high-pitched sounds or voices?'

'Not at all. Just went dead.'

'Well, we can be relieved at that. So now we are back on the secure line. Do continue about young Prince Bertie.'

'Just for security, Saxe-Coburg.'

'And Gotha.'

'Fine! Melissa, as I was saying. Top crisis here. '

'What crisis? Prince Albert gone AWOL?'

'Worse. Hijacked! Kidnapped. ISIS already claiming the heist.'

'Christ!'

'Indeed. He was waiting by the school gate at St Peter's Prep school, Vauxhall. When the usual motorcade arrived with the security bods. But they were fake. Ersatz. Bogus. Phoney. Cars same make, same plates, same number and colour.'

'Bloody hell... excuse the French...'

'Quite! Young Albert, and our escort for him, Lieutenant Martha Hare, RN, both taken. ...I say Melissa. Not the sort of stuff we can deal with over the blower. Can I come to see you Tout de suite?'

'Sir Samuel, the touter the suiter. Tricky stuff. You've alerted the crisis team, upped the security level and rounded up the usual suspects, to coin a phrase?

'Yep. But we need to talk Turkey. And I shall need your bods on to it. Is that David Brand still around. Smart chap. Just his cup of tea, ISIS and all.'

'Great minds! Thinking just that myself. I'll have him here when you arrive. 11.15 suit you'

'On my way. Toodle Pip'

'By the way Brand is working under cover as Dick Barnes. I'll send you a briefing note

'So Long! ... Natasha! Get Brand here. Immediate. Top security.'

(Later)

'Ma'am, Sir Samuel is here and I have put Brand in the waiting room.

'Natasha, show Sir Samuel in, then.'

'Welcome, Sir Samuel.'

'Sam. Please!'

'Some kettle of fish.'

'Quite so. I saw Brand is waiting. Shall we have him in now rather than repeating all the briefing.

'Fine by me. An old hand. And close to ISIS and their acolytes. Fluent Arabic. His bods on the inside now and he ... Natasha. Ask Commander Brand to join us, please.'

'Good morning, Dame Olivier and Sir Samuel. Something up? Nothing trivial I suppose from the classification used?

'Sir Samuel, do bring Commander Brand up to date.'

'Well, let me see Commander, to be brief, the second-in-lineto the throne has been kidnapped by ISIS. We want you to find him.'

'This morning?'

'No Brand. This afternoon as he was leaving his school in Vauxhall. Oh! That is together with his armed escort, Lieutenant Martha Hare. Know her Brand?'

'No not personally but she has a good track record I believe and a crack shot.'

'Indeed. But can you find them quick before we all have egg on our faces and a top rate international shambles on our hands.'

'Well, Sir Samuel, should not be too much of a problem. I do believe the Royals all carry LTEMI GPS tracking devices. Some now even have the micro mini SZOREND.'

'Even the children?'

'For sure Sir. Especially the children. Hidden in heels of shoes, sewn into clothing, Apps on mobile phones, watches. There is even one that has been used in dental implants. Let me check the latest Royal briefing I have here… Let's see. You say Prince Albert.'

'Yep.'

'Wow he has five. Four with 48-hour battery cover and one with solar and motion recharger. One concealed in each shoe heel, a third in his GPS watch, a fourth in the cartouche of his writing pen, kept usually in his pencil case, it says, and a fifth in a dental implant during the recent filling of a tooth. All come in the standard British military encrypted GPS tracking adapted for short messages and alarms encoded with two-way speech and texts in the latest models. I take it your team will be on to all that Sir Samuel and already getting his location'

'Right! Indeed. Let me see.'

'This is not the first stunt with Prince Albert, isn't it, What! I seem to remember it was a woman who infiltrated the school and was, happily, arrested before she found her target. Bonkers. And still in preventive detection awaiting psychiatric reports, I see, on my mobile.'

'Melissa, the Royal security team have already homed in on one signal located in Heathrow airport Terminal 4 and are closing in. Brand it's Operation Royal alert.'

While Sir Samuel, Dame Melissa and Brand were following the action text reports, the security team at Heathrow were moving in fast, checking a flight about to leave for Qatar.Within 30 seconds of detecting the locator alert, a team was racing from the Met Heathrow security unit SO18 in their Armed Response Vehicle (ARV) with five armed personnel were securing the boarding lounge. Then they found a young boy of Albert's description escorted by two heavies about to pass through the boarding gate. One of the heavies leapt the barrier and the other whisked Albert off his feet to hand him over. At this moment he was confronted by the boarding gate staff and the armed patrol. There was alarm and panic amongst other passengers shouting and diving for cover. One woman in the army patrol, drew her light weight semi-automatic Glock 17 Gen4 pistol from her Kydex IWB thigh holster. She raised it, calling,' Freeze!'.

Another with a G36C semiautomatic carbine cocker her weapon aiming at the heavies and called insistently for them to lie flat down with hands stretched sideways. She used her X25 taser and some pepper spray to immobilise them. The whole incident as being filmed from the patrols' helmet cameras and from the boarding area CCTV. Pictures were streamed by wire to Sir Samuel who shared them with Dame

Melissa and Brand. The whole rescue took less than three minutes by which time the whole camera coverage was being replayed on screens in Dame Melissa's office.

'Nice work, that patrol,' exclaimed Sir Samuel, high fiving Brand. 'It seems, my dear Melissa, that the second-in-line is now safe and sound and will be taken post-haste to Windsor to be reunited with his parents, who are staying there with the King Charles.'

'There will be a full Inquiry on how we came to be in this mess.'

'Sam, if this is ISIS, I will put Brand on to it to check through his networks. Not the first time they ISIS have been on to the Royals as trophy booty and for a King's ransom. Foiled again. It seems. Brand any thoughts?'

'The Prince of Wales, Prince James is actually closely monitoring Royal Security, following his stint of extensive briefing on all MI5 and MI6 matters, anticipating his more active future role, as his father King Charles III hands stuff over to him. It's a younger man's job really,' Sir Samuel concluded, breathlessly, 'I could just do with a brandy and ginger, what?'

'Hold on!' Retorted Brand, softly, I think it's not over yet. The escort has not yet reached Windsor. Albert's tracking devices have been found in the pockets of the heavies stripped from Albert's clothing.'

'How many devices, did they say, Sir Samuel?'

'How many, Spencer?... Four devices. Please repeat! So, just four.'

'That, Sir Samuel, probably leaves the dental implant device still operating, but probably with a very short range and life.'

'Spencer! Any signal still emitting? There is probably a fifth device.'

'Spencer, the army captain in charge of the patrol, says, just a faint signal, with a possible location moving towards Slough...'
'Brand any ideas?'

'Very odd! Strange! Not their usual modus! Sir Samuel, can you check the signal of the

ISIS claim for responsibility. There is a newly agreed code-word.'

'That will be at our HQ at the start of this escapade. Hold on I'll check… Yes, it seems the code word was in Arabic for which the given translation is Medina.'

Sir Samuel checked through his texts from his HQ.

'Yes, here it is in Arabic. المنورة المدينة

'Hm! That Sir Samuel is most interesting. It reads Medina al Munawwarah. Which means literally the Enlightened City. But as I recall the revised code word is Yathrib, in Arabic بِرَّثِ. Which was the original name of the city before the Hijrah, that is the Muslim migration from Meccah. So, we have a problem here. The code claiming it is an ISIS job is false. So, who is using the old name for Medina, and why? Perhaps not to trick us, but to tell us something?'

'Maybe, Brand, to tell **you** something.'

'Indeed, Dame Melissa. Indeed. I have it. It could be a link to my old friend Tamin bin Jibril Al Thun, in Qanar. Educated at

Sherborne, Harrow and Sandhurst. I met him when I was lecturing there on post-Bletchley cryptography. In our brief conversation there he referred to Medina by its original name, which I did not know. He rebuked me for not boning up on Middle East History especially as it was in Yathrib that the Muslim migrants became the peacemakers between warring Jewish tribes and established the Harem, meaning a place of peace.'

'Peace! This seems more about war.'

'I think, Dame Melissa, we shall find this is not about war, but about marriage!'

40.   **The Marriage Market**

It was some two months later, Maryam was dozing with David, in deck chairs under the boughs of the old ripening giant Doyenne de Comice pear tree, in their garden at Sheer; they sipped sherbet to cool the head, that Maryam had made that morning. They were watching Sara barefoot, practicing croquet on the tennis lawn, in her long summer skirt and light lacey top, casually revealing her ripening shape. Maryam whispered softly to David, 'You know my love, what you should be doing now for her...?

'And what would that be, my darling wife?' He raised his head from browsing the Foreign Affairs Magazine, catching just a glimpse of Sara's, blossoming youthful figure and multicoloured toenails, resonant of the Russell College pennant she kept on her desk.

'Perhaps more driving lessons for her, as I know she can't wait to take the Jensen for a spin, down the country lanes?

'No, my sweetheart, what every father needs to be doing for a growing daughter.'

'You have me there, what on earth are you musing on?'

'Her future. Not so far from here, my love, she will need a suitable marriage partner and fathers, elder brothers and grandmothers are the best informed for setting out on the search, before she gets caught in an adolescent mush.'

'Perhaps crush is the word you were looking for. But she is so terribly young.'

'Never too early. I saw the gardener's boy giving her the twice over.'

'That snotty nosed adolescent with acne! And more than just the once over!' He smiled at her courageous English.

'Indeed.'

'A dead end there, I think. Maybe I better offer some fatherly advice.'

'Advice! Take charge! And make up a short page.'

'Short list, I think, my dear, but she has such a mind of her own.'

'Aisha was betrothed to the Holy Prophet when she was just seven. '

'That was a different era, a bygone culture.'

Maryam put down her sherbet, staring hard at David.

'David, do take charge on this, I beg you, It is your very duty and a safeguard for Sara. Do you want her to try eloping with a local motorbike mechanism?'

David's mind strangely jumped back to the Heathrow affair.

'Talking of marriage plans, dear, It seems that …

His mobile rang.

'Brand here.'

'The Palace here.'

'The Kabul Palace Restaurant in Francisfield?

'No, Sir, Kensington Palace, his Royal Highness, Prince James would like to speak with you.'

David put his hand on the phone.

'Maryam, I have to take this inside.'

She smiled at David, nodded and went back to her sherbet, watching Sara, with her lovely skirt, waltzing across the lawn, her bare feet in the rising stalks of daisies, like confetti flowers for weddings. Days of joy ahead for Sara, she mused.

As Sara was joining her under the pear tree canopy, and sipping some of David's glass of sherbet, which had an aroma of fresh wild strawberries, picked that morning at dawn by the slope of the ha-ha, David reappeared.

Is my full-dress naval uniform here or in Cambridge, can you remember?'

'I haven't seen you in that for quite a time, Dad. What's the occasion, or is it hush hush as ever.'

'No, it is official, though at rather short notice for a conferment ceremony.'

'Who's conferring what?'

'It seems I have been awarded a gong. Commander of the Victorian order.'

'What did you do for King Charles Vic, then, you ain't that old are you, Dad, come on', chipped in Sara.

No, it's for that kidnapping palaver, at Heathrow, and little Prince Bertie, and there is a special audience with Prince Al Thun; oops sorry, His Excellency, Tamin bin Jibril Al Thun, Emir of Qamar.

It seems that the deal is Al Thun is buying a squadron of the latest Augusta Westland AW189 helicopters for air-sea rescue around Qamar, Prince James is co-ordinating the contracting recruitment and training – oh! and there is special project on sharing technology with Qamar on solar power systems and finally there is a deal for a royal engagement. Which is all rather wicked, Sara!

'Oh! Top! Yer! You'll soon be on to page 2 of the chat line, Dad!'

'Cos, the Heathrow affair was a hoax, really. A set up. A training day devised by Prince James to test the security systems. He enleagued his Emir mate Al Thun to provide the mock up vehicles and chauffeurs. Bertie was in on it and even carried a toy Glock 17 pistol which could fire blank caps in a thigh holster under his shorts. His personal escort was also briefed not to use any offensive weapon. Fine so far then: it went haywire. Al Thun bless him had other ideas. He was playing it for real. His phantasy was of a Royal marriage with his youngest daughter, using Bertie as bait. '

'Crazy!'

'All hush, hush of course, Scout's honour, DYB, DYB, DYB.'

'That's where I came in.'

'Dad to the rescue, dah, dah!!'

So, I must be in my Sunday best and off within the hour, they are sending a car.

41. Conferment

Sara and Maryam both fussed around helping David get dressed for the ceremony, brushing and ironing his uniform, polishing his buttons and shoes 'til they gleamed like mirrors. They took photos at the front door of Pear Tree Cottage, and waved as he left in the official car with a driver in Naval uniform, who opened the rear door of the limousine and saluted him smartly as he stepped towards the car. The girls giggled and both saluted with their left hands as he sped away.

David did not recognise the driver but noted the ribbons on his chest which denoted active service and as he had moved from the rear door to the driving seat, he had a slight limp, which could have been from a battle wound.

'Active service then Petty Officer?'

'Yes Sir. I'm Hatton, Sir. I try not to talk about active service, it, brings back memories I would rather forget.'

'Know that feeling too, Hatton. Lovely evening to be driving in the countryside. Been with the Prince long, then?'

'Ever since I was disabled from my ship, and opted for this rather than discharge on medical grounds.'

'Interesting assignment?'

'It's OK, but on high security with the prince himself, and his family. Lots of protocol, but then you would know about that Commander, with the line of work you have been on.'

'They briefed you then, Hatton?'

'Well yes Sir, but your fame rides ahead of you. Quite a name you have below decks. Sir.'

'A name.'

'Yes Sir, they call you Braveheart Brand down below and relate all kinds of stories, no doubt many embroidered a tad, of your daring-do.'

Brand pause abruptly at this point. On this mission was he playing under his cover as Barnes or back again as Brand. All rather confusing. He better play along with Hatton and the prince and see what emerged. Either way it would be tricky.

305

'Yes, well, P.O., fantasy and reality are two quite different things. You will know, from your active service, most of the time you're just waiting around for something to happen, playing games like Uckers and Final Theory.'

'Uckers, Sir, careful with that word these days, you might get a funny look if you asked for a round of uckers. The Navy's changed a lot below decks Sir, with the lady tars. The Bridge players also can't ask if it's time for another rubber. Know what I mean Sir?'

'Quite! Well, here's to our wives and sweethearts.' David advanced.

Hatton added, the favoured response, 'And may they never meet!'

David chuckled as the chauffeur eased through the gates of Middlecroft, but. forever wary, David spotted a white van with what seemed to be Albanian number plates, almost concealed opposite the entrance under overhanging willow trees, as they cruised up the winding driveway, beneath the cedars of Lebanon, towering over the neatly trimmed rhododendrons, gliding to a halt beneath the portico, with the Prince's Royal coat of arms and his Royal standard at full mast.

Hatton alighted and came with a sprightly step, despite his disability, to David's door to welcome him to the estate and to announce him to the Royal butler, 'Commander David Brand.' David struggled a little to adjust his gold braided cape and to return Hatton's salute, smoothing down the creases of his dress uniform, straightening his dangling medals, as the great doors of the house swung open and a smart young naval lieutenant stepped forward, saluted and greeted David.

As David moved towards the door, he bent before Hatton to adjust his shoe lace and whispered, go out now Hatton, check that white van by the entrance. An Albanian military number plate I think, Blue stripe, AL and MM followed by 435 PU, I think. Let me know, later. Check with Interpol, Manchester, and if necessary, the National Central Bureau of Interpol, Incidence Response Team in Lyon, France. David stood up, with a smile, adjusted

Hatton's medal ribbons, and turned towards the great door.

'Commander Brand', announced the young Lieutenant, 'you are most welcome to Prince James' country estate. This way Sir.'

David returned the salute, took a deep breath to quell his nerves, stepping forward at a brisk pace, he noticed Hatton driving off towards the front gate. He mused thoughtfully. 'What is a van from the Albanian military police doing here?'

David, raising his head, followed by the lieutenant, moved into the pillared hall, where his braided cap was taken into a cloak room. Then he was guided through the hall and into a panelled reception room, with tapestries of famous battles and life-size equestrian statues, gilt framed portraits of the prince's forbears. David was served with a choice of cocktails by livered staff amidst a distinguished assembly of military officers.

A naval captain approached him.

'Commander Brand, I believe. I am Captain Ian Breckenhill: HMS Raleigh.'

'The submariner training school in Cornwall?'
Hm! We were there but have now been shipped
to the Clyde, and bloody cold it can be up there
after our rather better digs in the south west.
Not so many tourists of course, wanting to take
snaps of the latest kit.'

'Quite! But more space I guess.'

'Indeed. Now Commander, may I lead you on
to meet the prince. Just a tip: Your Royal
Highness first and then, Sir.'

'Yes, Quite! Do lead on Sir.'

David found himself in another grand
room, probably a ball room, he thought, with its
polished floor, a décor in gold and blue, with an
orchestra loft above, where a small band was
playing quietly songs from the shows and
Viennese waltzes. The long room had a range of
French windows that opened out onto a paved
terrace, a lawn and beyond that, highland cattle
grazing on a meadow replete with buttercups
and clover in full bloom.

'Your Royal Highness, may I introduce to you
Commander David Brand of the Royal Navy.'

David bowed his head and took Prince James' proffered hand.

'Commander Brand!'

'Your Royal Highness!'

'It is a special pleasure to meet you, Brand, after the Heathrow palaver. We are greatly indebted to you, my son and I, for handling the contretemps with such aplomb. Indeed, you prised us out of a veritable balls-up! Now, Commander, after the conferment,' he lowered his voice with a sterner look, 'I will need to see you privately to discuss a little discrete mission we have for you, right up your street.'

With that the Prince turned away to greet other guests. David felt his spirit failing as he had rather expected this ceremony was to be a prelude to a well-earned retirement. The last thing he wanted now was another mission, which seldom turned out to be little or discrete.

As the music faded the assembled distinguished guests and the platform party were ushered into a ceremonial room. A trumpeter sounded a bright welcoming voluntary, the chief usher announced the prince in elaborate terms quoting his full official name and titles.

'My Lords, Ladies and Gentlemen, pray be upstanding for His Royal Highness Prince James Arthur Philip, Louis, Prince iof Wales.'

The formal part of the evening went like clockwork governed by strict protocol. Except when the prince pinned on David's gong, he lent forward and whispered, 'They call you Braveheart Brand, I hear.'

'I believe they do.'

'Well Braveheart I shall be inviting you to be my equerry.'

David was lost for words, and feeling trapped.

'May I, Sir, have time to think about that.'

Later after a further informal gathering in the reception room, the naval captain asked David to follow him.

'His Royal Highness would like a word.'

In a private lounge, in another wing of the house, Prince James greeted David warmly and explained the equerry role was designed to cover David for other personal duties to the prince, which would require David to have the highest security clearance. That would be arranged. There would be two tasks, first, a covert, deep penetration into the Middle East through the Qamar link, to locate a breakaway ISIS cell with a biological weapons' store and research station working on more deadly variants of the COVID virus for tactical warfare. The brief is to trace the location and propose options for turning it for UK and western use before the Russian and Chinese oligarchs get there first. David would be briefed on the progress to date. His task was to ensure the West, in this decisive field of biological weapons, was up to the mark and keeping ahead.

David grasped a new reality. The prince, with his military training, was following in the footsteps of his great Uncle, Louis Mountbatten, with a role at the heart of the secret service. David wondered whether this would embrace a newly developed form of the combined operations executive, in joint service warfare planning. Or was he a step or two ahead of himself. He quickly refocused on the rapid briefing

The prince resumed, with David becoming both intrigued by the complex tasks ahead and his inherent caution about being dragged down a pathway with no exit. If he declined, he would be already compromised by knowing too much of the deep secret objectives and the main players. The briefing continued apace. Second, David was to be engaged to check out the credentials of the proposed marriage between the youngest prince Malcolm and the even younger daughter of the Emir of Qaram. David thought, was this part of a wider plot to draw the Royal Family into a new twist in the Middle East circus? And third, David would be assigned to work with Professor Geoffrey James on tracking the alleged link of clandestine heroin trade from Afghanistan to the top brass of MI6 itself.

David winced: that was the killer job, suspicions triggered deadly enemies, and such enemies had the most secret ways of suppressing the message and the messenger. As a little light relief, the prince's right-hand man, Captain Breckenhill, explained the pay-off. For the duties David would have a team of assets, locally recruited and whatever other assistance he needed. The jobs were to be all top secret. Pay? He would retain his naval rank and pay, plus the usual special expenses. Breckenhill flashed a list on the usual special operations. David noted, more than generous allowances, non-attributable, tax-free. And David surmised the notes would be in specially printed currency of any country required, with no doubt sequence numbers, directly traceable to each player, as a guard against clandestine use. David would be next week having a full briefing from the prince's team and with a special commission working on these matters, personally reporting to the prince and his father, the King Charles III.

The audience ended as quickly as it had started and David was whisked away by the captain back into the reception room as the other decorated celebrities were departing. David was feeling pale, deeply depressed and silent from the conferment with his medal and this extraordinary briefing, as a hand touched his elbow.

'Hatton, it's you!'

'Yes Sir.'

'And?'

'You were right, Sir. Albanian, and their military Police, just pulling away now, so I came back to brief you. A covert listening van, no doubt linked to mikes on someone here or previously embedded.'

'Covert bugs!'

'Yes, Sir, probably throughout the whole place. Found two. This Mongiti bug on a flower pot by the reception area terrace and this stuck to the window frame of the prince's private lounge where you were being briefed.'

'You're so sharp at this cloak and dagger stuff, Hatton, well done, first rate!'

'Strange though, Sir, as we had the whole place screened last night. It was clean.'

'The clean-up team? Infiltrated! Trust no-one, Hatton: chapter one page one, in our little handbook. Report all this to the prince.'

315

'Done and dusted, Sir.' Hatton pointed to his earpiece, and turning over one of his medal ribbons he disclosed a minute microphone.

'He said, you would know how to handle this. Sir.'

'Quite! Let's go back to Sheer. And Hatton I want you to be on my team?

'Done and dusted by HRH this very moment.'

On the way Hatton briefed David further on his findings. The white van was being deployed from Albania in line with a bilateral link between the UK and Albania military police for counter-terrorism training. It was co-ordinated through NATO and the Organisation for Security and Co-operation in Europe (OSCE). All part of an international response to the threats posed by returning migrants from the Middle East after the fall of ISIS and the dispersal of Da'esh and El Qaeda.

Hatton, continued, 'the military police vehicle was, according to INTERPOL's National Central Bureau in Manchester, originally part of an international training exercise for detecting terrorism activities, but had been hijacked on

Salisbury Plain, last Tuesday, during the exercise, by an unknown armed group, possibly mercenaries, who overpowered the Albanian crew of five, abandoned them in a remote cottage, taking the vehicle off. This is the first sighting of it.'

'Intercepted SIGINT from the vehicle,' H\tton continued,' warns that it may have been involved in a break-in, taking on board biological and chemical weapons from a top-secret army laboratory within Porton Down, where our brain-boxes have been conducting animal and human trials on weaponised nerve gases. '

Hatton paused, watching David's reaction. David tried to absorb all this, as he fingered his new gong and pondered on the offer from the prince. His depression deepened as he tried to work out how he could explain any of this to Maryam and Sara, without divulging official secrets.

'Thanks Hatton. We are getting into a right old mess, I can see.'

'All part of the job, Sir. Never a dull moment with this lot. Not so much time for uckers now, I'd say!'

'Quite! Makes me yearn for some time at sea, where everything seemed so much simpler. Just a battle against the natural elements in a good ship stout and free.'

'Back to the old-style active service? Not for me, Sir! Invalided out of that, I was, weren't I? Scars I'll carry all my life, body and mind. No thanks, Sir! Besides, all this is very intriguing in'it, Sir. Keeps us on the qui vive, know what I mean? What do they call it, Cloak and dagger stuff?'

'One more step closer to the grave, Hatton. Just one more step and we know not when it will come. Very sudden. No doubt. You say chemical weapons? Biological weapons? Once had a trip round Porton Down. All very jolly chaps, who told us nothing. 'Can't say about that... hush hush that room. Very hush hush that lab. No-one's been allowed in there since that Novichock stuff was detected on those poor Russian dissidents. Off limits.'

Hatton continued, 'A bloody deep pool of mad scientists with their favourite deadly toys. Put that in a thriller, no one would believe you.'

'Still using it they say. Got a mate who works there. Horribly disfiguring and mostly fatal. Well; here we are at Sheer. I'll drop you, Sir, and be on my way. Give me a buzz when you need me: here take a card.'

'So long! Hatton. Take care. Be good to work with you!'

David regretted that as soon as he had uttered it, as he was desperately in the need to go AWOL on the whole thing. A defector at large, with his dahlias, looked just then by far the best option.

Hatton lowered the driver's window and with a cheery wave imitated the piping of the captain on board.

Maryam opened the front door and immediately spotted that David was in a dark mood and tried to comfort him.

'How's the marriage fancy fayre then, sailor?'

David groaned.

Sara rallied round.

'What's all this about a marriage market.'
David looked up at her blossoming figure, half
girl half woman.
'OMG, Dad, not that. Not me for sale. Not now.
Please Dad. Just not ready for that. Not in the
least. Terrible distraction from what I am now
up to.'
'Indeed, you are so young, my love. No, not
marriage. Not now. And with this, this gong,
I've decided to chuck it in, to tend my dahlias,
and of course my two sweethearts.'

'What? Defecting?', Maryam was
trembling. 'Do that… and you will be dead by
next week-end. Prime target by all sides in this
crazed world. No David, darling. Not that. I
could not bear that, now that we have you back.
No!' She fell to her knees her hands spread in
supplication, her face distraught, tears flooding
down her cheeks.'

42.   A Friesian Bull

Two months later.

From: cm@ukintel.org
To: ZM@ukintel.org
Take the defector out. ASAP. He's on to us.
MO

As dawn broke an unmarked white van moved from a south Thames parking lot, reserved from special missions. On board three heavies in Batiskin Cobra Plus ultra-light helmets with the modular protective attachments for full facial protection, SAS style combat dress in heavy flame resistant clothe, body armour, respirator masks, soft soled black calf length boots, GPS radios, and ultrafine powder of Novichok nerve gas in sealed canisters in their Russian standard issue Raid Backpacks. Well protected against all risks of their own assault and any retaliation. But they were not prepared for a Friesian bull.

Their white Albanian van, with its three-litre engine, cruised into the north-circular road, at Park Royal, and sped off to the motorway link for the M3 to intercept their target south of Salisbury. They were well tuned to David's rakish classic Jensen, using the GPS location bug they had had an agent plant under the rear wheel casing in Francisfield market carpark three weeks before. Maryam and Sara had been shopping for new outfits for the summer, at their favourite Chloé Khan's Eastern Fashions. They were unaware the Jensen had been tampered with.

Earlier another mercenary forces' unit, ostensibly on a training exercise, had planted a remote-controlled explosive device against a cattle fence on the country lane which Sara regularly used from Sheer for her week-end driving lessons, with David and Maryam. The aim was to release a large pedigree bull from his pasture adjacent to a field of young cows, ready for breeding. The bull would then have access, all day, to the tasty young cows, by trotting a hundred yards down the lane and pushing open a rather rickety five barred gate, which had been left just ajar. Mihai, a Romanian immigrant farm worker and part-time undercover field agent had helped set up this ploy.

Timed right the bull would be in the lane as Sara approached, she would have to brake, allowing the white van contingent, close at hand, to intercept the Jensen and eliminate the defector and his family. Then they planned to speed to a rendezvous at the motorway service station at Liphook on the A3. They would abandon the white van and their equipment and return in a silver-grey Toyota Rav 4 to a safe house in Chichester, to be debriefed by Zac on their mission accomplished. In the event the white van was superfluous. The Friesian bull, Bernard, was all that was necessary. Though not quite.

I suppose you might think it is rather a pity that David gets bumped off out of the blue, when we might have been all cruising towards a happy ending. But that's life which has usually rather muddled conclusions, if any at all, except for the final heart beat and the cold grave, or the superheated incinerator. So, there it is.

The enemy proves to be the Bernard the Friesian bull, with head down, he pushes, and pushes, with his two-tonne weight, and some more, splintering the fence. The bomb proves to be a dud. He trots across the country lane, against the flow of traffic, jauntily for his size, in full anticipation of being well contented with his maiden herd of cows,

Sara is driving. I do not hold that against here, though she is still technically underage and has to have a cushion to get a good view of the road ahead and stretches a bit for the pedals in her father's Jensen Interceptor with its 7.2 litre engine. He is determined to be officially retired, now with the naval rank of full Commander and an OBE and the Victorian medal for his services. Sara has a photo of him with the prince and the medal in a smart little blue box. He will never look on that again.

They are taking their usual back route from Sheer to give Sara some quiet driving practice. They do actually have some L plates up as a warning to other motorists: which the Bernard the bull, sadly, does not seem to notice: nor Sara, the bull, Barnard, as she is chattering twenty to the dozen and turning her head to check that David is still awake. Maryam is strapped in the back seat not quite approving of this underage driving lesson.

'By the way darling daughter, Maryam thinks we should be looking for a husband for you.'

'What rubbish, I'm scarcely a woman yet – Not one of those child brides. OMG!'

'Well darling,' adds Maryam, 'I do think you should have some instruction and convert to our faith. Despite the evidence to the counterside, Islam is a faith of love, charity and forgiveness. Think about it. We both pray that you will.'

'Hmm! I will give it some thought, but not before we negotiate this nasty tight bend.'

Sara manoeuvres though a hairpin bend, towing and healing with aplomb, turning her head to get her father's approval. He smiles sleepily. Maryam sees Barnard first, who is followed by a small herd of cows. The eager bull is checking them out for feasible mates and blocking the entire way through.

'Sara! Watch up!'

A screech of tyres and the smell of scorching rubber: then thud, thud, and a tinkling of broken glass as the bull encounters the headlights with lowered head. David hits the wheel with his fist to sound off the Jensen's blasting horn. Sara turns the fast car to avoid a collision, but runs it up the bank of the pleached hedgerow into the field beyond. The car rolls over. There is a fire.

Maryam escapes. She cannot prize open the front door where David lies trapped by his seat belt, engulfed in smoke and flames. His door is clamped shut as the car has rolled onto that passenger side. Sara shouting for help unclips her seat belt, pulls herself up (no air bags in these classic cars), shoulders the door open and jumps free of the blazing car, stripping off her smouldering clothing as she tries to heave the car upright. Some cows are down. The bull bleeds profusely from a glancing blow. Maryam screams for help, sobs appealing to Allah. A following car halts and calls for emergency services. The fire catches the hedgerow. Some cows are on fire. Others scatter trying to evade the flames. Barnard, staggering under his weight, moans in pain and for the loss of his afternoon fun. The classic Jensen suddenly explodes scattering metal and scorched body parts back across the country lane and further into the uncut meadow profuse with buttercups, clover and margarites, their sweet aroma masked by the blackening fumes from the Jensen's fuel, oil, interior fittings, their summer clothes, human and animal flesh.

Finally, the emergency services arrive. Firemen douse the last vestiges of fire and smouldering remains. One young woman paramedic finds a blanket for Sara to cover her exposed body who is in great pain from the disfiguring burns. The ambulance takes Sara and Maryam to the Francisfield hospital burns unit. The police find David's wallet and note his identification, immediately calling their HQ, who contact the Admiralty who in turn reveal the news to the duty officer in David's unit. Commander David Brand, Braveheart Brand, is dead. The white van was not needed and the heavies return to Zac in their safe house in Chichester.

A family Muslim funeral is followed by a low-key official naval memorial service. Melissa Olivier expresses her admiration for David's naval career. A formal statement mentions his distinguished contribution to the Intelligence services.

This was to be the corrupt peak of Melissa's career. The rest was downhill to a grisly end. Dame Melissa Olivier, CBE was the first female head of MI6. She was the daughter of a Merchant banker. Her mother was a curvaceous brunette, much sought after daughter of the Anglican Biskop of Bath and Wells. She had rather played the field after coming out at 18 and the belle of the London ball season. Melissa had followed her style and indeed was endowed with her mother's lovely figure which she used to great advantage. Melissa had boarded at Wycombe Abbey

School. She had had a brilliant academic record and excelled at sport, becoming Head Girl. Her mother wanted her to take the veil, following in her own father's footsteps in the priesthood. Melissa rebelled, rather by accident as it turned out.

It was at the school annual ball, where a young handsome Chairman of Governors, took her aside for a chat. He was, he explained, a senior member of the National Intelligence Services' Committee and had his eye on here for joining the team and could secure her a place at Russell College, where she could read Maths and cryptology. Not to put too fine a point on it, she was very willing for him to be a sugar daddy. Over the next three years she became embedded in the calling, and after gaining a double first she signed on at MI6 and cynically slept her way to the top.

Her accelerated promotion surprised no-one as she rapidly became the charming, witty and endeared escort to the great and not so good. She was always elegantly dressed and sensationally undressed in the top hotels and penthouse flats and stately homes. She was brilliant in her skills in Intelligent work, master of numerous languages, a ruthless manager and social climber. For this there were many rewards. Melissa was the recipient of a wealth of perks from her distinguished and rich admirers vying for her hand and much else that was so agelessly alluring. She had by the age of thirty taken irrevocably the primrose path to the everlasting bonfire. She enthusiastically sought the company of one of her class at Wycombe, Priscilla Khan, the daughter of an Afghan warlord who first introduced them to recreational drugs and wild young boys.

She was habituée of the Bouji's night club, Mahiki's opposite the Ritz and the Raffles club in Sloane Square, where she teamed up with a like-minded group of Sloane Rangers, who like reckless libertines, trod the deadly path of dalliance at night and into the morning. Yet in the day she was the undisputed mistress of all she surveyed with none who feared her more than those top dogs whose beds she had enjoyed and who worried about the cards she held for personnel blackmail. Her toll so far had been five cabinet ministers of a variety of political persuasions, five British colonels, seven foreign military generals, and a clutch of Olympic champions having been detected as infiltrated agents by foreign powers.

As head of MI6 Melissa might talk seductively to them at night but she carried a big stick in the day, with not a few having tasted her pitiless capacity for weird forms of unmentionable humiliation at the least sign of their faithlessness. She had once had ideals, a patriot, cleaning the stables of treacherous filth. But her virtue had become eroded with time at the top. Temptation she could seldom resist. She found bit by bit that she eluded detection with her charm. She was never challenged and power held her in a relentless grip as she found the system awaiting her commands however bizarre.

Rich foreign corrupt playboys were all, more or less, her regular diet, in the course of duty: her real preference, however, was for young, vigorous beachboys, masseurs and pool attendants, whom she enjoyed as a personal hobby on the side. Such relaxation she believed was a critical factor in her remaining on top. She believed she was untouchable, until her downfall, which was quick and decisive.

David had been in her black book for some time. The funeral was one of Melissa's typical ploys to tighten the leash on her subordinates. She had had her suspicions about David and he had lost her favour when he had encountered her in an embrace with the Afghan ambassador.

After the funeral Maryam was distraught as she arranged for daily prayers for David calling in the local Imam. She and Emma visited Francisfield hospital, daily, morning and evening to check Sara's progress. Sara exchanged texts with Trueman, who was much more into the real-life plot than he seemed at the Soirée. He was becoming rather more than just a friend.

Melissa closed her file and began burying the loose ends. She took a month's leave to Guyana recruiting fresh young vigorous houseboys there. Frank Trueman was working with a forensic auditor tracking a paper trail from Kabul, linking, London and finally Guyana listing Desmond, Melissa and Zac as the prime suspects. Trueman also had gathered some fresh evidence from interrogations of a Taliban defector that they, and other junior staff had been complicit in a series of security breaches. This web of material supported further suspicion that the diversion of heroin payments was part of treasonous wider links with the Taliban military secret service leaking documents, before, during and after the British involvement in Kabul.

Then Zac was found dead in the Chichester safe house along with the three heavies from the white van, some days after the funeral. They were all registered at Chichester hospital as COVID19 deaths, delta variant. The nerve gas containers had leaked. Trueman had the safe house cleaned and the containers deposited at Porton Down. Just two more on his hit list.

43.   Emma takes leave

After the car accident and David's death, while Sara lay seriously injured at Francisfield plastic surgery unit, she felt profoundly guilty and deeply depressed. Maryam tried to comfort here. It was just an accident after all. But the plea, you are not to blame, seemed to make Sara weep all the more and her slim body became enveloped in emotional convulsions which drained her.

'Why him and not me. Why should I be saved,' she moaned and cried out again and again. 'What sort of God of mercy is Allah? He wanted me to marry a good faithful Muslim and to convert. But now, now, now, how can I, when he is gone, in that burning car. Just dust! Ash and burnt fragments, was all that was left of my lovely Dad. Nothing really to bury. How can I go on with this secret foolish life of lies and deceit?' Maryam wept too, for her lost mate, so gentle and kind.

Maryam called Emma to come to see Sara in the hospital ward, side room, where she had been put to avoid upsetting the other seriously ill patients in the intensive care area. A young house officer came. He talked to Sara who agreed to have further sedation which he said would help her sleep, which was important for her recovery. Her treatment was going well and she would have some surgery involving tissue expansion grafts which should help to reduce the extent of visible scarring on her face and neck. This would be explained by the consultant who would be doing a round the next day. The treatment would take some time over various sessions. But now she should rest and he would return later to check that pain relief was working well.

The houseman, Hew Williams from Cardiff, was a well- known a Rugby Union Welsh international. He said this was sometimes embarrassing for him when some patients, especially keen rugby fans preferred to be seen by him rather than the registrar or the consultant. He was very popular in the hospital, tall, handsome muscular and the very epitome of a rugby attacking full back. He chatted with Maryam and Emma when he discovered they were Sara's nearest relatives. He was very friendly and explained the issues and prognosis in simple terms, in his lilting Welsh accent. He was amazed when Maryam explained she had been in the same car in the accident, escaping with just a few bruises. They laughed about the poor bull and the herd of very sad young cows who had missed their fun.

After his gentle chat with them, Hew Williams strode off from the ward to do his outpatients, with a bundle of medical records under his bulging right arm. Emma confided to Maryam she was pulling out Russell College and the cloak and dagger stuff. She had had enough and could see that it was a dead end for her.

'The worst of it is, you can never tell who are your friends. Suspicion is rife. David was lucky to have survived so long after all the attempts on his life.'

Maryam was supportive and sympathetic to Emma. So difficult losing an elder brother. 'Just one life. And it is not long. Do what will use the best of the gifts Allah has bestowed on you. Emma. Avoid the evil paths of this world and prepare for the next. I am praying for you, and for Sara every day, that Allah in his great mercy will spare you for a good course in this life and save you from the cracked paths that lead to the eternal fire.'

Emma smiled kindly and thanked Maryam for her love and advice and pledged that should indeed avoid the cracked paths, a very good word that!

'Do help Sara in the same way, please. She is so fragile beneath her outward show of boldness, and tormented too by unwarranted guilt. I really do fear for her life ahead. She will need great help over the next few weeks, to confront the future after all that mess to her face and neck.'

In her passing from sleep to restless waking, Sara increasingly felt the pain not just of her wounds but of the loss of her father. They had become very close and he had been her dearest friend. He was the only one she could entirely trust. Sara felt it her duty to her father to clear his name, to heed his advice, and yet she knew should could not carry on his type of work.

Emma visited Sara many times over the coming weeks as she was completing her series of plastic surgery treatments. She remarked upon the huge improvement in her appearance and her mood. With brilliant plastic surgery and carefully applied make-up the worst features of the burns had been suppressed. Emma tried to get Gordon II to come down and provide some male distraction from Sara's moods which whilst improved still swung too often to the dark side of life. Sara did not want to be taken in hand to overcome this difficult transition. Sara knew the disfiguring facial and burns would never just look like minor blemishes. She was scarred for the rest of her life and that was the retribution imposed on her for killing her father. She was the driver and failed. She fell out with Gordon II who tried to make light of her physical and mental torture. He left for Scotland finally distraught.

Emma was feeling guilty at having put too much hope in her stepson and the burden that she had attempted to transfer to him. Emma once more sought comfort with Gordon I on bird island in The Seychelles away from it all, leaving Sara with Maryam who was completing her days of mourning for David supported by a coterie of ladies from the local Mosque who had befriended her in her time of need. Yet Maryam felt uneasy

338

about the future. Were they completely safe from David's enemies, or did they remain on a target list in a contract that had been put out for their lives? She did not confide these fears to Sara who was slowly recovering from her terrible ordeal: she pondered them in her heart and was kept awake at night with bad dreams which even her most fervent prayers could not dispel.

44. Guyana

Melissa Olivier sits in the lounge of the five-star GOLD Crest Hotel in Alberttown Guyana, sipping chilled fruit cocktail and chatting quietly with a companion, playing with black olives. Local Guyanan friends come to speak to her. She laughs, delves into her Gucci handbag, handing out wads of newly minted currency. She tips the waiter lavishly as he serves fresh drinks and appetisers and kisses her houseboy as he waves to her goodbye. He has done his stuff copiously. It amuses her that much of the currency is British forged for agents, in the long line of the SOE station 14 at Briggens. 'About time that was designated as a National Treasure and turned into a museum, like Bletchley Park,' she thought as she riffed through another wad of Bradburies.

Her companion in a wheelchair indicates it is time to go. 'It is', says Trueman, who whispers to himself softly, with a faint smile, 'All we need now is for Audrey Hepburn to kiss her.'
'What?'

340

'Nothing, Ma'am, I was reflecting on a scene from a very, very old film: but then you are not Alec Guinness.'

Now, Trueman, surprisingly, rises from the wheelchair and walks off briskly, winking at the waiters.

'Amazing what robotics can do for you with some AI blended in!'

Melissa Olivier ruefully smiles to all, waves generally to the other guests and staff. She takes in hand the arm of the wheelchair, when it is apparent that she is handcuffed to it and under arrest.

A waiter helps Melissa into the wheelchair. She is evidently disabled, with plaster on both legs. She had been shot by the secret police attempting to evade their brutish hands. She attaches herself to an oxygen mask and leaves the restaurant guided by a young waiter, in obviously increasing discomfort and embarrassment. Frank Trueman is waiting for her by the maître d'hôtel. She nods to Trueman, speaking with difficulty lifting the mask away for a brief moment.

'You know, young man, I would prefer to end it in the comfort of my private suite and avoid all the fuss back in Blighty. And by the way, whatever happened to our friend Geoffrey James.'

'Ah, James. Yes, he had been in our bad books for some time, like you, Ma'am. But he did not try to dash away, after we showed him the instruments of torture.'

'In the Tower?

'Indeed ma'am, the very place. Then he just spilled the beans on you all and will be entertained at her Majesty's expense for a very long, long time... Sorry, you said you want to avoid the fuss and expense, Ma'am?

'Indeed. Something quick.'

'That can be arranged, Ma'am, if you wish.'

Frank whispers to the waiter to take her to her room.

'Goodbye then Ma'am, I think you will sleep more easily with this with a shot of gin.'

He hands to her a little antique pill box.

'Rest assured you will be collected in the morning.'

Frank Trueman takes the next plane back to London.

Relaxing in his first-class lounger, after an à la carte menu of lobster Thermidor prepared by the on-board French chef, Trueman muses on his mission.

'Two down, one to go!'

A short obituary notice is shown in the Times of London recording Dame Melissa Olivier's distinguished diplomatic career and her untimely death, on vacation, after having had an unexplained car accident returning to her beach house. She had been left disabled and in need of life support. She died peacefully after a short illness arising from her injuries.

Postscript

Extract from Sara's diary

Trueman is solid, Came over to see me on Saturday, to console me over Dad. Gr8. Whatever happened to his robotic wheels? Nearly back to his former self. Not all the equipment tested though. OMG, not after me? He said that the evidence FWIW that Dad was a defector and traitor was all chicken feed concocted by Melissa and Zac and Desmond who were her lame dogs in an omnishambles. Dad was a real one, despite all the palaver. He told me about Guyana where Melissa held court with the booty from the Taliban deal. Her swag millions came from the stash of heroin that was intended as a nugget to the Taliban top dogs for a better deal on women and border security. He was awesomely vague about the details, but she's quite done for now. She'd been at Uncle for years with her cut outs Zac and Desmond. A SWAT team gathered the rest there, all in at midnight – a black op. Zac was a throwaway. Just leaving Desmond.

I chatted about my future and his. Frank said he had brought a friend, I thought go tell Traylor Swift, but it was legit. None other than Gordon II, again. I tried to be grateful, Not that I wan2 find a mate now, cuz I need to keep going on the grind. We laughed it off. Am I right ladies? But it's solid to know someone cares, or what. Oh! Taaas! Trueman also said Geoffrey James, is in the can all part of the deep state plot. So as Dad said, trust no-one, not even yourself. Just makes me wonder, What's his game, Trueman? Maybe genderX Don't want to be cuffed. But, seems a real one. Though not quite a dreamboat, even walking.

So, there we are. Sara begins a new life, releasing herself from Russell College and seeking new ways to use her talents. Trueman gave her a contact in UNICEF, a new project working with refugee children from war zones. She links up with Maryam to open a new chapter looking forward with hope into the future and then maybe conversion to please her dad.

Sara and Maryam are just finishing an informal game of tennis, without a net on the lawn, flush with daisies and clover, that needs cutting and rolling. They sit under a willow tree on a rug. Maryam gently comforts Sara about her wretched facial scars from the car explosion. She takes from under the rug a present wrapped cutely in silky paper with scenes of the blue Mosque in Istanbul and ties of silver and gold. Inside Sara finds seven delightful veils and jokes with Maryam as whether they are enough for a naughty dance and realizes they are chosen as a subtle way to cover her lower face and chest where she was so badly burned.

They laugh and embrace with tears running down their cheeks in a seamless frolic in such cherished moments when they have no dark cares for their fate on that blissful afternoon. Maryam urges Sara to give some thought to marriage and to reconsider conversion to Islam, both which would have pleased her father. Sara ponders this in her heart. Maybe, her destiny is with the Red Crescent sister organisation to the Red Cross and saving lives rather than being involved in a world of secret spies, lies and deniable assassinations.

They leave the lawn, Maryam carrying the rug and Sara the gossamer light presents, skipping softly barefoot in their cool summer dresses, bustling through the front door of Peartree cottage, to make a simple salad lunch, with feta cheese, olives, cucumber and avocados, and a hot freshly baked cottage loaf, before taking an afternoon snooze together.

Amidst their delights they do not see that white van with its new UK number plates. There are three heavies aboard, all masked with Desmond in the driving seat still carrying his lifelong grudge. He says a little prayer for Father Patrick. The white van passes slowly past the garden gates, pulling up quietly under the shade of the cedars of Lebanon, with the scent of fox heavy in the air, with the contract killers ready....

Sara dozes, listlessly, lying beside Maryam, in the tranquil upstairs double bedroom, chasing away fragments of those crazy dreams that still haunt her sleep, climbing all those stairs in that place with no windows … an eccentric gardener with strange boots…

Anyways, let's get after it!

The End

Author's notes

Settings

The story begins in Copenhagen, moves on to Budapest, to Cambridge, diverts to Halifax Nova Scotia, Canada, with its penultimate fatal scenes in a country lane in Sussex and a luxury hotel for wealthy Western women in Guyana. The story closes with Sara and Maryam relaxing in their blissful country cottage in Sussex, but closely shadowed by an expert gang of contract killers.

Characters

The cast includes:

Sara Brand, a naïve child prodigy in mathematics and cryptology liberated from an early life misdiagnosed as autistic.

David Brand, Sara's father, an agonised defecting British triple agent, seeking atonement for his past grim, clandestine life in espionage.

Maryam, an enslaved ISIS captive forced to work as a tutor to convert ISIS prisoners to Islam under pain of savage torture or death.

Sandra Brand (née Jones), David's first lover and wife, now unhappily married, who yearns for return to her former professional life in aid to developing countries in Africa.

Melissa Olivier, head of MI6 intelligence services, who formerly ran 'honey trap' projects to turn enemy agents into counter intelligence work.

Emma Brand, David's feisty sister, linked to British espionage and living with her hugely satisfying Nigerian partner Gordon.

Desmond Archer (Catholic born Patrick Murphy), adopted as a child by Protestant family but develops as a covert Catholic rebel from Belfast and wily henchman to Melissa, watchful for chances to get revenge for British misrule during the Irish troubles and the assassination of his parents.

Zacharia Owain Glyndwr, a fervent Welsh nationalist, and trusty henchman of Melissa.

Frank Trueman, a disabled BBC security adviser and undercover British agent and self-confessed tiddlywinks champion on ice, who befriends Sara.

Igbal, Ismail and Abdulla, Muslim Cambridge students, befriending David

Prince James, first in line to the throne in UK, father of Prince Albert.

Prince Albert, son of Prince James,

Sir Samuel Cecil, head of Royal Protection Service for Prince James, Prince of Wales.

Natasha, former honey-pot KGB agent,

Dr Brian Summerfield, forensic pathologist at Cambridge Institute of Criminology,

Dr Martin Greensmith, on-call pathologist Kerry Hospital, Ireland.

Prince Tamin bin Jibril Al Thun, crown prince of Qamar.

Dr Henry Williamson MP, Chair of UK Intelligence Security Committee

Professor Geoffrey James, a young academic working for MI6, holds the chair in cryptology at Russell College, Cambridge.

Author's reflections

This elliptical thriller is a moral tale of people entangled in their thwarted idealism. The principal part is of the young teenage prodigy Sara. Her story unfolds through her frank naïve diaries after she has been liberated from a secluded infancy marooned in profound deafness, misdiagnosed as autism. Her deep love for her father, David, tempts her to follow his footsteps in the secret service, aided and abetted by his feisty sister Emma. The first entry in her diary is of a recurring nightmare in which she is in continual vain search for a meeting in a convoluted building, with a helical stairway, where the bottom floor is at the top. This is a metaphor for the whole tale of people trapped in a web of delusion, confusion and deceit.

Despite her brilliant mind, Sara lacks the moral compass to steer her safely through the ensuring maze of dilemmas leaving her contemplating ending her days.

David, her father, is haunted by his distasteful past in pitiless espionage, but caught in a rollercoaster journey from which he seems unable to escape. Sara discovers this and tries to save him from his enemies.

Sara's nightmare is a counterpoint to the twists and turns of the plot and the unravelling of characters whose destiny is confounded by continually changing alliances leaving no-one sure who is to be trusted. David's maxim, trust no-one even yourself, leaving us guessing whose side he is on and that of the other main players embroiled in ambiguity of a fast-moving story line. There is no real beginning and the end leaves us in suspense.

David's enemies are not demonic villains. They have their own forms of idealism, but become engulfed in the temptations of power, using it for their own personal ends and not for any higher purpose. Frank Truemen represents the saving grace of morality in a labyrinthine system of conflicting powers in international affairs.

Maryam has a key role in interpreting the tale. Who does she work for is as complex as her journey as a captive ISIS slave in Syria to the peace of Pear Tree Cottage in Sussex. She starts as a captive of ISIS working to turn other captives to the ISIS cause of world domination. Maryam knows that ISIS sees this as noble quest, bringing better order in a troubled world in line with traditional Islamic principles. But Maryam rejects this creed seeing Islam as a faith of love, charity and forgiveness. She is the moral compass in the story. Her role is trying to weave an honest way through the complexities and moral turpitude of a religious war and of the shifty practices of espionage, to find atonement for her loved ones, David and his wayward juvenile prodigy Sara.

David's role in the narrative is to expose the nefarious practices of the spy trade of which he is a continual victim. Can he find the strength to escape the forces of retribution and a love strong enough to survive?

Can Sara avoid following in his footsteps in the tragic path of espionage, and find love and forgiveness in another setting for her brilliant mind? Can they all be freed from the evil web that can enmesh those engulfed in the trade of espionage?

Made in the USA
Las Vegas, NV
12 February 2023